Magic Hands

Magic Hands

Jennifer Laurens

Grove Creek Publishing

Grove Creek Publishing

A Grove Creek Publishing Book/ published by arrangement with the
author

MAGIC HANDS

Printing History
Grove Creek Publishing edition / Sept 2006
Grove Creek Publishing edition / Feb 2009
Grove Creek Publishing edition / Feb 2011

Cover artwork by: Jennifer Johnson of Sapphire Designs
http://designs.sapphiredreams.org/

Book Design by Julia Lloyd of Nature Walk Design

ISBN 1933963972
Printed in the United States of America

For Rachel

ONE

Senior hall was a river of students shouting, laughing, and shoving. Rachel stood at her locker, turning the knob, casually scanning the busy hall for one person.

He was at his locker. To her shock, his beautiful face turned and those bottomless brown eyes were fastened on hers. Her heart stammered. Should she smile back? Ignore him? Flip her hair? Walk away? Walk *his* way?

Cort Davies was looking at her. Even a glance from the guy was enough to send most girls into a head spin. Though he was completely hot, he broke the number-one rule in Rachel's book of must and must-nots for guys – he was a superficial jock.

Too bad, she thought and decided it was time to walk the other way for that very reason. She couldn't stand jocks, even though a few like Alex had hung in her circle. Most thought they were it-boys—that the world and everything in it revolved merely to serve whatever whim they possessed.

Not her type.

But she could admire the physical specimen of a jock – no problem. Yeah, they didn't get much better than those manly-built guys like Cort when they were in their football uniforms. It was cool to watch the boys play hard—all that

1

sweat and pumped testosterone. She could admit she went to games to watch the players.

Rachel hadn't thought of a code name for Cort yet, but she would. What to coin a guy with wild, dark hair surrounding the face of an angel? The only thing she could think of to describe the rich coffee color of his eyes was espresso. *Xpresso?*

Rachel and her friends had been code-naming hot guys at Pleasant View High ever since they decided they didn't want to stop talking about those same guys just because they were in the same classroom or someone might overhear.

Today Cort's khaki pants were just baggie enough. His deep chocolate sweater just snug enough that his sculpted chest and taut arms caused her stomach to flutter. She was a face girl, and his was, well, beautiful. He had a cute ski-jump nose over lips full and wide, set in the frame of an angled jaw.

She wanted to sneak another peek but didn't.

Cort was in all of her honors classes, which meant he might not be the typical back-row, thumb-sucking jock like the others. She'd heard him make some pretty intelligent comments.

Don't fool yourself, she thought, and fought the urge to glance back, see if he was somewhere behind her. He was so cute, wouldn't it just be stoking if he really was intelligent? If he lived for something more than girls, weekends and sports?

She had to look.

He was right behind her, so close if she stopped, she'd be in his lap. His bevy of guy friends surrounded him: Carmel, Brownie and Sunshine – all named by her, Ticia, and Jennifer for various personality or physical attributes.

Cort's magnetic brown eyes were on her, as if he'd been watching her the whole time. Suddenly she felt naked. She heard the conversation he was having with his friends, smelled the mixed scents they wore.

"So, not today?" Sunshine asked him. They'd named Eric that because of his sunny blonde hair and surfer stride. Rachel slowed so they could file around her. Cort smiled as he passed, brushing his arm into hers.

She had to smile back.

"Yeah," he answered Eric. "Not today. I gotta go job hunting. I'm broke, dude. Hey." The 'hey' was for her, and his espresso eyes sparkled with sugar when he nodded.

He left his scent in the air—something citrus and spice. It wound her blood up tight. Cort Davies, she thought as she followed him into class, now it's my turn to watch you.

Cort needed a job—bad. The Purple Turtle, the greasy burger joint with the bright purple roof and stone walls was already crawling with students. Subway, Quiznos, Walmart— nobody was hiring. Cort had even secretly called the Daily Herald to see if any paper routes were available. At seventeen, it'd be pretty embarrassing for a high school senior with only four months left before graduation to be out throwing papers before dawn but he'd have done it. He got the same answer there he'd gotten at every other establishment – No.

Which left him the newest business in town: Chachi's Nails on Main Street with its **Here Job Open** sign propped in the window.

He went in, choking on the waft of strong fumes that hit him. Then he stood, staring into the faces of five little Asian women. The place was narrow and deep, its walls covered in crimson wallpaper with gold designs all over it. Posters of colorful women showcasing their equally colorful nails hung on the walls. Small tables lined the sides like a school room. Each had a hot lamp, small pots with brushes, and other stuff he didn't recognize. The women were dressed in shiny satin dresses with high collars. Fancy buttons ran down the sides of their dresses.

A woman stood from behind the desk nearest to the door and tapped over to him in flat, black shoes. Her eyes smiled like setting suns on her round face.

"Welcome, welcome." Her accent was thick as chop suey. She looked him up and down and gestured to the empty salon where the four other Asian women immediately scattered to their tables.

"You need manicure?" she asked, tugging out one of his hands he'd tucked safely in his front pockets.

"Uh, no." He pulled it back. He was beginning to sweat in his leather letterman's jacket.

"I Miss Chachi and welcome to my salon. You want massage?"

He bristled. "No. I—" He jerked his shoulder toward the sign in the front window. "I want a job."

Miss Chachi's eyes squinted even more as her smile grew.

4

Cort noticed the women in the back gather, huddling and whispering as they watched.

"You do nails?" Miss Chachi asked.

He shrugged. He'd do just about anything. The smell was overpowering and again he coughed, looked around to see where it was coming from. "Sure, I can do nails." *How hard could it be?* He glanced down at her long fangs. Jeez. With their red slashes and sparkling diamonds they looked like a pair of his mother's earrings. But he could paste those pups on.

Miss Chachi hooked her arm in his and led him into the salon where the other women quickly surrounded him with gleaming smiles. They chatted in a language he couldn't understand, openly checking him out.

Maybe I should run now, he thought, shifting anxious feet. But Miss Chachi's grip was firm and she was rattling off to the women.

"You live here in Pleasant View?" Miss Chachi asked him.

"Yeah."

"You know people here in Pleasant View?"

Cort shrugged, trying to stay cool. "Yeah." He'd lived in Pleasant View all of his life. His mom was a lawyer for the city. They knew people. And he was quarterback for the Pleasant View High School football team. That qualified him for a yes. "I know tons of people, yeah."

Miss Chachi looked at the women, chattered something then beamed up at him. "You know lots of females, yes?"

Cort's face heated. He'd been voted Mr. Viking, been homecoming king, had a date every weekend. That qualified him to say, "Yeah."

Miss Chachi squeezed his arm. "You hired."

That was it? The sweat that had glazed Cort started to cool him. He had a job.

Miss Chachi sat him at one of the tables, then sat opposite him as the other women, Misu, Tiaki, Jasmine and Abby, introduced themselves. All spoke with the same, clipped-chime accent as Miss Chachi.

The women huddled over his shoulder. Mixed with the nose-scorching smell already filling his head was something candy-cane sweet, like incense, one of them was wearing.

Miss Chachi grabbed his hands with a tug Cort hadn't felt since football season when the coach had yanked his jersey because he'd been out of order. She placed them palms down, on a paper towel that lay on the table between them. The light was white hot.

"Now," Miss Chachi began, still smiling. "Nail is very easy to learn. Lady like pretty nail and that's what we do, we make nail pretty for lady. You can do that?"

He thought of the glue-on nails he'd seen his little sister try. "Yeah, easy."

This seemed to please Miss Chachi who nodded, massaging his fingers absently. "Very good. I show you how." She kept hold of his right hand efficiently opening three pots, one with pink dust, one with white, one with a clear liquid so strong, Cort gagged and instinctively jerked back in his chair.

With a tight squeeze to his, Miss Chachi kept his hand in hers. Her smile dropped. She shook her head, wagging her finger under his nose. "No gagging."

"But it stinks." He gagged again. The women laughed.

She pulled his hand hard and he went still. "That stink is the scent of money. I told you, lady like pretty nail. This stink make nail pretty. Pretty nail make money. Now," she smiled big again, happy to have finished with the reprimand, "if nail is natural, like this, you buff with sander."

She reached for an electrical appliance that looked like a stainless steel toothbrush. The buzz reminded him of the dentist. When her fingers held his pinkie finger prisoner over the white paper towel, his eyes grew wide.

What the? Her eyes honed in on his pinkie as she brought the buzzing thing with the spinning sander toward his nail.

He jerked his hand free and stood, causing the hovering women to step back and whisper. "What are you doing?" he squeaked.

"I do your nail. Show you how nail is done."

"My nail? No way." He shook his head, shoved his hands in his pockets, slowly backing away from the table. That's all he'd need, one red, glittery fang hanging off his pinkie. The guys would kill him.

Miss Chachi was around the table and under his nose in a blink. She reached for his hand but he kept them both anchored in his pockets. "You need to know how to do it," she said and pulled.

He shoved his hands deeper. "No way. I—"

"You cannot work at Chachi's and not know how to do nail. It easy, I show you."

"Show me on somebody else," he said.

She nodded, then she coiled her arm around his. So

did Misu. He glanced frantically at the two of them as they guided him back to the table.

Misu sat, nodding at him with a smile. "You watch," she said.

"Yes, it easy." Miss Chachi sat across from Misu, signaling to the other girls to surround him in case he tried to run. "You watch."

Miss Chachi took Misu's hand. Misu had medium-length nails with white tips and diamonds. In a blink, Miss Chachi had Misu's pinkie nail and ripped it off. Misu let out a little yelp. Cort froze. Her face showed shock for only a moment before she took a deep breath and the shock was gone.

"You start with bare nail," Miss Chachi began, revving up the sander again. She sanded the nail bed. "Sand smooth."

Cort watched Misu carefully to see if she was in any pain but the girl didn't flinch. That rip had to have hurt. Inside his pockets his fingertips absently ran over his own nails.

He looked at the dainty black-haired woman holding Misu's nail captive. She appeared too cutesy to be deliberately mean. This was just business, right? Miss Chachi then painted a foul smelling liquid over Misu's nail bed and blew. "This primer. It make acrylic stay. You must use primer."

Cort nodded.

Dipping her brush in the pot of clear liquid Miss Chachi said, "This the pink." The thick mixture clung like a bulb at the tip of the bristles. "Watch carefully now, beauty-man."

Beauty man? Cort's face grew hot. What had he gotten himself into? Smoothly, Miss Chachi brushed the pink onto the nail and as she brushed, the powdery ball turned into

8

something thick. And made a nail.

"Wow," he muttered.

Miss Chachi smiled as she shaped the nail into a square with the end of the brush. "Yes. Pretty nail. We no use white today. For you, no use white. We keep it simple."

Cort nodded, glad to have any allowances he could in this foreign feminine subculture.

"After nail made, let dry. You move onto next nail. After dry, sand again." Miss Chachi grabbed the sander and it buzzed. Cort grimaced, checking Misu's calm face for any signs of discomfort but the girl sat like a statue.

"Feel." Extending Misu's hand toward him, Miss Chachi indicated he was to touch the nail for himself. He did. The texture was smooth as plastic.

Miss Chachi then lifted a four inch buffer. "Then buff. Feel."

Sure enough, the surface of Misu's nail was like silk and Cort nodded. Easy. He could do this. No problem.

Miss Chachi squeezed gold oil onto Misu's cuticle and massaged it in. "Last step, oil cuticle. Massage in, like this."

After the treatment was finished, Misu rose from the chair. Miss Chachi spoke, "Client wash oil away. If oil not washed away, it make polish bubble and look bad. Lady not like that. They complain, come back, demand new nail. It cost money." She chirped out something in another language and the women nodded, muttering replies.

Misu came back, sat and placed her hand out for Miss Chachi who took her finger again. "Most lady want color. They pick color, you paint. You know how to paint?"

He nodded. He'd painted plenty; the garage door after
the pep squad had spray painted *Hottie* across it in brilliant
blue. The living room wall after he'd kicked a hole in it when
he'd been chasing his sister who had stolen his journal and
read some of it. He knew painting.

"Misu have white tip. We air brush. Watch. It easy, you
see."

Miss Chachi held a small, gun-like contraption in her
fingers and arranged a paper shaped crescent over Misu's nail
as she sprayed white. When she removed the crescent, there
was a white tip. Misu held her finger up with a smile.

"Cool," Cort said.

Laughter broke out around him and he smiled at the
little women who began chatting.

Miss Chachi stood next to him and Misu was replaced by
Abby. "Your turn."

Cort looked at Miss Chachi through tentative, wide eyes.
"Me?"

The women laughed again. Miss Chachi nudged him
around the table and into the warm seat. "You. Do it."

Cort's heart pounded. He looked at Abby's hands splayed
on the paper towel before him, at her bare nails. Paint, pink,
nails. Women. Could he really do this?

Four faces peering over Abby's shoulder with smiles told
him that he could.

TWO

Cort walked down the hall a new man. He figured he was the only guy at Pleasant View High School who could do nails. Not that he'd advertise his new skill. He was still pretty tentative about the fact that he did nails for a living.

Well, *would* be doing nails. He'd been working at Miss Chachi's for one week now and had yet to do nails on anybody but Misu, Tiaki, Jasmine and Abby, all of whom had kindly allowed him to do multiple practice sets, until Miss Chachi gave her nod of approval.

The tiny little woman was a tyrant when it came to nails, he decided. One week into employment and she was cursing in her native tongue, which he'd learned was Vietnamese, every time he screwed up.

All of the girls who worked for Miss Chachi— as she wanted them to call her— were Vietnamese. They were a close-knit group, but he could tell they were all trying to make him feel part of it.

It was kind of cool being the only guy working at the nail salon. The girls all liked him and because they were older, they treated him like a little brother all gushy the second he walked in the door from school.

He laughed, and pushed open the door to Miss Tingey's

classroom. Yeah, he'd had enough experience with girls to qualify himself as a stud. Girls had always liked him and, he'd always liked girls—except his sister, who he loathed most of the time. She seemed to exist only to torment him.

But girls in general were pretty fascinating.

He sat at his desk, nodded a greeting at some girls staring at him before he looked at Miss Tingey, writing the journal entry of the day on the blackboard: How ego affects our actions.

Miss Tingey was hot. Cort tried not to be obvious with his glances. She had great legs; all the guys knew that, even talked about it. He liked her because she was one of them, not condescending like some of the teachers or administrators at the school.

Cort slapped palms with the only guy in class he talked to, Kevin Mackerel. Being smarter than most of his friends had its drawbacks, leaving him in honors classes without anybody to hang with but second choice friends like Kevin.

Kevin plunked into the seat next to him, his shaggy blonde hair looking like he'd just rolled out of bed.

"Dude, sleep in?" Cort asked on a laugh. He himself never came to school unless he'd showered, had to shave, which didn't happen too often thankfully, and he was casually coordinated.

Kevin yawned and sat back, extending long legs. "Was up chasing freaking deer out of my mom's garden all night."

"*What?*"

"Gotta put up some stakes with hair and dried corn on 'em." Kevin wiped his hands down his heavy-eyed face. "So I can get some sleep."

Cort shook his head. "Hair?"

"Hair freaks 'em out. Or so I hope. Until then, I'm chasing them around like a freaking dog, freezing my butt off so my mom's scotch pines don't get eaten."

"Just put netting over them." Cort knew deer could ravage a yard in one night if certain plants weren't protected; their own yard had bushes wrapped up tight for the winter to protect from foraging.

Kevin shrugged. Miss Tingey started class.

Cort looked over where Rachel Baxter usually sat. He hadn't seen her come in, something he watched for because she walked like a goddess. He'd never seen a girl walk like she was saying come get me and you can't have me at the same time.

Her desk was empty when the bell shrilled. Then the door opened and he sat forward, his heart thumping. When she came in, the room hushed. Even Miss Tingey looked at her.

Today she wore blue jeans with random cuts and slices in the denim. Her black shirt had sleeves that hung long and weepy. She looked hot in black and wore it all the time so Cort figured she must know it.

Her hair was the color of mink and just as shiny and silky hanging down her back. He wanted to know what it felt like and his fingertips rubbed together absently.

She had the bluest eyes he'd ever seen, like the sapphires his mom had. Rachel's eyes were big and round and slanted in a way that reminded him of a kitten. Somewhere inside of him warmed fast. She looked like a kitten, but a wickedly hot kitten you weren't sure would rub against you or claw your eyes out.

She never greeted anyone when she came in. She sat, primly erect, ready to listen. Part of that untouchable thing, Cort guessed. She took school seriously and lucky for him, they shared all of their honors classes.

It was safe to glance over because she'd never look at him. Why, he didn't know. Every other girl stared at him. Why didn't she?

Suddenly, he was looking into those deep blue cat eyes and his breathing stopped. Before he could give her one of his studly nods, she looked back at Miss Tingey.

"You have five minutes to write your journal entries," Miss Tingey said. The class immediately began to scribble in their notebooks.

I have no idea how ego affects behavior, Cort thought with aggravation. He'd missed his chance to impress Rachel and was pissed. *I don't even have an ego.* He drew lines. *Egos are for celebrities and rich people. Sure, we have money and live in a big house but, so?*

He began to write.

Why don't the chicks we like ever like us back? Even as he wrote, he knew the question was gross exaggeration. He'd had lots of girls he liked, like him. But things were different now. He was different. He was a senior, going into his last half of the year and for the first time, he didn't have a girlfriend because he'd had enough of arm candy. Nobody interested him.

He glanced over at Rachel Baxter. Something tingled deep in his chest. Her profile was perfect. Her flirty nose was small and pretty, and to admire another angle of those pouty lips—any guy would be blind not to notice how chewable they looked from any perspective.

Sweat broke under his armpits, around his collar. He shifted in his seat, gnawing on his pencil eraser. He had to get to know her, that was all there was to it. But they'd never hung in the same crowd.

His was the hot crowd. Hers was small and elite. In fact, she had only two close friends, associate babes Ticia Levin and Jennifer Vienvu. The three of them were legendary for always being in the center of the most random group of guys; guys that ranged from band geeks to computer geniuses, to a few select jocks. Most of whom Cort had ever hung with. Now, he was jealous of that. The girls were most definitely babes, but exclusive babes that, to his knowledge, no man—not even those in their random circle, had been able to crack.

What would he find if he cracked that elusive Baxter outer shell? He'd heard she was raucously funny, brilliantly off-beat, a total stud-woman. But he found it hard to believe, watching her primly writing in her notebook. It would be cool if she was, like she'd show only that secret part of herself to those really close to her.

"Mr. Davies," Miss Tingey said, startling him. "Share your thoughts with us."

Cort sat up, nervously tapping his pencil on the desk. His page had nothing but a grumpy complaint on it. "I need more time," he said.

"Miss Baxter," Miss Tingey said and Cort forgot finishing his own work. Rachel was going to speak.

She cleared her throat. "Ego is an invisible if not integral part of personality," she began. Cort loved the sound of her voice, cream and spice. "Every person has one, whether they know it, or admit it, or not. It's what drives us to do what we do, say what we say for social acceptance. Some people's ego is worn on the cuff, like your basic cheerleaders or jocks. They're too shallow to know better. While others carry theirs deep inside."

Cort's face drew tight. What the hell was she talking about? He didn't like her assessment and cleared his throat, bringing eyes to him. But not hers – she kept reading her notebook. "In fact," she went on, "jocks and other superficial people model their egos after what they think is socially acceptable, rather than exploring who they really are."

Miss Tingey had that smile of satisfaction she got whenever somebody hit the intellectually stimulating mark. "Very good, Rachel. Anybody agree, disagree?" Cort raised his hand because her words had hit him like an arrow. "I disagree."

He was ready to shoot an arrow back but when those mystic-blue cat eyes slid to his, his arrow drooped. "Uh, well, it just sounds kind of generalized, that's all. There are exceptions."

He couldn't believe it, Rachel's left eyebrow slowly lifted and her blue eyes were wickedly playful. The look shot another arrow straight to his gut. It lodged there with painful pleasure. Her lips curved into a smile.

"Of course there are exceptions," Rachel said to him, the cream of her voice spilling into his veins. "Though I have yet to see any."

Was she daring him? If she was, it was freaking hot and he'd take her up on it— absolutely.

"There are some generalities about ego and behavior, for sure," Miss Tingey said. "When attacked, an ego defends itself, feeling like its position must be justified, even if that position is inaccurate. A person whose ego does not drive them will be secure in their motives, and not jump to defense every time something is said that threatens them. Finish up your entries."

After class, Cort trailed a cool few feet behind Rachel. It was hard to listen to Kevin who walked with him down the crowded hall, droning on about deer, about how much hair he'd collected from his mother's hair brush. So Cort focused on the easy sway of Rachel's hips, the way she occasionally flung that long, silky hair over her shoulder, filling the air with the smell of something sweetly tempting she washed it in.

He had to talk to her.

"So I've got about a zip-lock bag's worth of hair now," Kevin muttered. "All I need is about four stakes, some corn cobs, which will be frickin' hard to find since corn season is way over, and—"

"Gotta go dude, catch you later." Cort positioned himself in the crowd next to Rachel. Their shoulders rubbed. Casually, he looked over. She was nearly as tall as he was, and he liked that. He could look straight into her eyes.

"Hey," he said.

She quickly skimmed his face and the act heated his skin. "Hey."

"Was that a challenge back there?" he asked.

She lifted a shoulder. She had the greatest smile he'd ever seen on a girl, not too wide because her mouth was small and delicate. But there was power behind it. "It can be."

"You think all jocks are ego maniacs?"

"So far."

"I'm going to prove you wrong."

"Yeah?"

"Oh, yeah."

She stopped and the crowd streamed around them. He felt eyes, heard whispers but didn't care. In fact, he relished them. *Let it be known I'm now hanging with this beautiful creature.*

"How are you going to do that?" Her voice oozed inside of him.

He had no idea, so he shrugged. But he'd spend the rest of the day and however long into the night he needed until he figured it out. "Just be ready."

Something sparkled just at her chest where she held her black binder. Her nails. White-tipped and the pinkies had a diamond in each corner.

"Hey, your nails look great," he said before he could think not to.

She looked surprised and held her hand out to look at them. "Wow, that was random. Thanks. But they need to be done again."

He swallowed embarrassment. "They look good." Then he glanced around. The hall was thinning, growing quiet. "Go to Miss Chachi's. They do great nails there."

Her face twisted in a look that made his stomach crimp. What had he done? Buried himself before he'd gotten a chance to take a breath? He wanted to die.

"I saw that place. It's new, isn't it?" she asked.

He nodded, relieved she seemed to ignore the stupid way he was talking about nails. "I gotta go." He started off, sucking in deep breaths, keeping his red face from her eyesight.

"Cort." His name had never sounded so great. He had to turn and look at her one more time. She was smiling and it eased his insides a little. "I'm ready for that challenge," she said.

* * *

Cort walked through the doors of Chachi's Nail Salon ready to do more multiple sets of practice nails. Or clean the sinks. Or sweep the floor. Or anything else he and the girls were told to do by the tiny tyrant. From the heavy mood of the place, the way the girls all huddled near the back, whispering, he knew something was up.

It was Miss Chachi's temper. He'd only heard her mouth off in Vietnamese and had no idea what she was saying. Now, she was mixing her rants with broken English. He stayed by the door in case he needed a quick exit.

She banged cabinets, clacking and stomping in red

stiletto shoes. Misu broke away from the whispering huddle of the girls and slid up front.

"What's with her?" he whispered.

"She very angry. No client in two months of being open. Very, very bad."

"What can we do?"

"She run ad, she flash light, open door wide. She pull client in from street."

Cort could believe that. The woman was strong in a deceptive way, kind of like a Chihuahua.

He followed Misu to the safety of the back where the girls stood, some filing their nails, others biting them, as they watched and waited for Miss Chachi's orders.

Finally, she slammed her last cabinet and looked over, her eyes honing in on Cort. He bristled. She tapped right over to him, her finger wagging. "We need client. You need bring client in. You beauty man, you know tons of people, you say."

"Yeah, I do, but—"

"No but," she snapped. "I hire you because you know people. Where are people? You tell me where people are."

He swallowed, shrugged and looked toward the big picture window at the front of the store. He recognized three girls from school peering through the windows and quickly moved past Miss Chachi.

"Hey." He opened the door and gave the girls his best smile. Bree, Megan and Shaylee, three of the hottest girls he knew—and they knew that he knew it. They returned flirty smiles, gathering around him.

"Hey, Cort." Bree tossed some of her long, blonde-striped

hair over a tan, bare shoulder. "What are you doing here?"

He glanced back into the salon, at the nodding grin Miss Chachi was sending him. "I work here."

The girls' eyes widened, they exchanged glances and giggles. "I told you," Bree said.

"She thought she saw you coming in here last week." Megan posed, extending one bronzed leg near Cort for his appreciation. It was the dead cold of early spring, but that didn't stop her from wearing her plaid miniskirt and short-sleeved shirt. "I told her no way."

Cort leaned confidently against the door. "Well, I do."

"You do nails?" Bree asked.

"Sure do—great ones."

"I'm having a set." And with that, Bree was the first to enter the salon with a flip of hair over her shoulder.

"Me too." Shaylee was fast to follow.

Cort grinned, and trailed the girls in.

Miss Chachi scurried up, all sunny smiles as Misu, Tiaki, Abby and Jasmine quickly filed to their respective tables and sat.

"Welcome, welcome to my nail salon." Miss Chachi extended her arm in invitation. "You are here for nails or massage or manicure or pedicure or—"

"Yeah." Bree nodded, looking around. "We want Cort to do our nails."

"Very good." Miss Chachi put her hand on Bree's arm and gently escorted her to Cort's table in the back. She sat her down in a chair with a pleasant shove.

"He do good nail for you. Cort!" She clapped her hands

and Cort was there, sitting across from Bree, his face blushing red.

Miss Chachi fluttered over to the other girls. "You want nail too?" They nodded, shifting awkwardly. "Tiaki or Misu can give nice nail."

"We'll wait for Cort," Shaylee said.

Miss Chachi took them both by the elbows and led them to the big, fat pedicure chairs. "You sit. Have free pedicure while you wait. Jasmine and Abby do good pedicure for you, you see." She assisted the delighted girls by setting aside their handbags and shoes, then helped them situate in the large, comfy chairs.

Jasmine and Abby were ready to begin before she clapped for them. They turned on the swirling warm water and gestured with their hands for Shaylee and Megan to lower their feet into the tubs.

Shaylee giggled. "Cool."

"I've never had a pedicure," Megan gushed.

Miss Chachi took one look at her feet and nodded, muttering something in Vietnamese that both Jasmine and Abby agreed to.

Bree sat forward with a flirtatious smile, both of her hands extended to Cort. "So, when did you start doing nails?"

Cort's hands were trembling. His first client— scary— but he could do it. She was only Bree, and they were friends after all. He took her hands in his. They were cool to the touch. "You cold?" he asked.

Her smile broadened. "Not anymore."

He tried to keep an air of professionalism. She wiggled

her fingers, rubbing them over his.

"You didn't answer my question," she said.

"About two weeks now." He started sanding.

"So, how's it going?"

He wasn't about to tell her how dead the place had been. "Great. Busy."

Bree glanced around at the empty tables. "Yeah?"

"Tell me if I'm too rough," he said, running the sander over her pinkie.

Because he was concentrating on her fingers, he missed the way she grinned and shot a look over at her friends.

"Did you see the way Carmen was dressed today?" Bree asked both girls, now having their feet scraped.

"Hideous," Shaylee said.

Bree whipped out a laugh. "Those scarves tied everywhere were just too strange. She looked like a retarded gypsy."

Megan nodded, watching Jasmine rub the scraper over her heel. "Like some gay fairy or something."

"I heard she asked Kyle to the dance this weekend."

"Nu-huh."

"Yeah. Can you see them together? Fairy freaks."

"She thinks she's so hot."

"When she's really just a loser."

"But then so is he."

"Totally."

The girls laughed and continued their gossiping.

Cort was shocked. He kept his head lowered, his eyes on Bree's hands and nails, but his ears were sponges, soaking up everything. He'd heard his sister talk about boys, life, and the angst of being a teenage girl, but it was nothing like this. He thought he knew these girls; he'd even hung with them on occasion. But he'd never heard anything more than flirty syrup from their mouths. This was black tar. Did all girls talk so viciously about their friends? What did they say when they talked about people they hated?

They didn't keep any of it quiet, he noticed. They laughed—loud, as if they were at a football game. Not that it mattered, the salon was empty.

"Ty's such a loser." Bree flung some hair over her shoulder. "I swear, the guy is so dense, he thinks I'd actually go with him after he's ignored me for three days."

"So you're not going with him to the dance?"

"I'd go." Bree lifted a shoulder. "But he's been so lame lately, and he's so careless, I'm just going to let him suffer it out."

Bree was dating one of the guys on the football team, Ty Morgan. As Cort began forming the first pink acrylic nail, he glanced at Bree. He used to think she was pretty cute but this was starting to bug him, the way she talked about people, his buddies.

"You talking about Ty?" To keep from being too nosey, he kept his eyes on her nail.

"Yeah. He's been a real jerk lately. It's been, like, three days since he's called me."

Cort often let that many days go by between communications of any form with a girl. Had he been wrong all this time? He stopped forming the last nail on Bree's hand and looked at her. "Maybe he's busy."

"So," she said. "We're, like, going out. That means texting if nothing else." With her free hand, she dug into her purse, pulled out her silver phone and pressed a few buttons. "See? Not even a message. Creep." She shoved the phone back.

Cort was confused. He knew Ty had a job, had gone from football team to basketball team and was throat-deep in senior stuff. "He's got practice after school, Bree."

He formed her last nail and she leaned over and hissed, "No matter what, I should come first."

"You go girl," Shaylee piped. Her toenails were being filed. "Careful there," she told Jasmine.

Cort looked from Shaylee to Bree. "But the guy doesn't even know—"

"—Exactly," Bree said, tossing her hair back and looking her nails over. She smiled sweet as corn syrup. "They look awesome, Cortie. You're amazing."

He almost rolled his eyes, too irritated with her to enjoy the compliment. He took her fingers. "I'm not done yet." He began to sand the surfaces.

"All I'm saying," he started, "is give the guy a chance. He can't help that he's buried."

"And all I'm saying," Bree's tone mimicked his, "Is that I should matter more or it's over."

"For sure." Megan held up one foot, wiggled red-painted toes. "There's tons more cocks in the barn."

Bree and Shaylee nodded. "Like Chad or Ben."

"Or John," Megan added. "Wait, he's with Jennifer now, isn't he?"

Cort nodded. "Since the play."

"That's gay," Bree said. "I wanted John." Shaylee jangled her bracelets before running her hands through her hair, fluffing it. "Oh well, Chad and Ben are plenty hot. I'm going for it if Derek doesn't ask me."

"Who you taking, Cort?" Bree smiled her white teeth deceptively clean and pure looking.

He shrugged but it was Rachel's face that flashed in his mind. He wanted to ask her. But after hearing these girls talk like dogs in a junk yard, he wasn't going to tell them anything. "I don't know yet."

Bree leaned close. "You could ask me. I may not be going with Ty."

"Maybe, yeah." He didn't want to hurt her feelings—if she had any. He kept his eyes on his fingertips, feeling the smoothness of Bree's nails. "You want color or white-tips?"

"That feels good, Cortie." Immediately he stopped, and set up to paint. "It's so cool that you do nails," Bree cooed. "You're, like, the coolest guy ever, touching girls and stuff."

"Yeah," Megan agreed. "The coolest."

Cort wanted to laugh. He had no idea that it was all about strategy, gossip and guys. Who was hot, who was an idiot. He didn't know what he thought girls were about. He'd never thought about life from a girl's perspective.

After he'd done all three of the girls' nails, taken their twenty-eight dollars apiece and their five dollars each in tips, he felt like he needed to fall into one of those pedicure chairs and sleep. His brain buzzed with the high-pitch of girly chitchat, Miss Chachi's enthusiasm for their very first sale, and the zipping hum of the sander.

THREE

Cort walked into his house and let out a sigh. Being home had never felt so good. The spicy scent in the air instantly comforted him. He'd often seen his mom look the way he felt—dead to the world tired—and for the first time he understood what it was like for her to go to work all day.

He dropped his backpack to the floor, peeled out of his coat and plopped on the soft linen-white couch in the living room. He wasn't allowed to set foot in the museum-quality room his mom had decorated and set aside only for guests, but he was the only one home so he took advantage and it felt wickedly good.

Until he heard somebody clear their throat.

His sister, Lizzie, was smiling through narrowed eyes. "Get lost," he told her and shut his eyes.

"Fine," she said. "I'll just tell Mom that her only son, who's old enough to know better, was sprawled on her favorite couch when she gets home in three seconds because she just called me on her cell phone and told me to open the garage door for her."

Cort jumped up. "You would." He straightened the pillows, fluffed the couch. "Garage door broken again?"

"Uh-huh." Lizzie followed him into the kitchen like an

27

annoying gnat. She sniffed. "What *is* that smell?"

Cort stopped and lifted his arm pit.

"Not *that*," Lizzie said, coming around to face him. She stepped close for another whiff before putting amicable distance between them again. "Like…nail polish."

Afraid his face would give him away, Cort went to the refrigerator and opened it. "Your nose needs an overhaul."

"No, that's definitely nail polish."

Seeing carrots and celery, surrounded by apples, oranges and bananas, he shut the door with a groan. He needed real food, chips, salsa, bean dip and cheese. "There's nothing to eat."

"Why do you stink of acetone?"

"Why don't you stick your head in a hole?" He rummaged through the cupboards. His mother breezed in wearing her usual navy suit, navy hose and navy shoes. Her briefcase was in one hand, her cell phone in the other, pressed to her ear.

"Yes, Celia. Fine. We'll talk tomorrow." She clicked off the phone and let out a sigh as she set her briefcase on the counter. Having caught Cort's food search she said, "Don't bother. I got rid of everything unhealthy."

Cort shut the last cupboard and leaned his brow against it with a loud sigh.

"What kind of mother would I be if I let my children feed themselves garbage?" she reiterated. "I might as well pull up the trash tote and plunk you both down in front of it for dinner."

Cort turned, folded his arms. His mother was on another

one of her jags. This time it involved food—what not to eat. Rarely had her various jags affected him. There was the time when she made them all rise at four in the morning just to go running together as a family – something about early exercise and family togetherness. That lasted until winter set in and her mascara-covered lashes had frozen like spider legs.

And the time she insisted they buy a hot tub for therapeutic reasons. Some study she'd read said hot water cleansed the spirit as well as the body. That had been cool, with extra benefits Cort snuck with his then-girlfriend. Until his mother started raising the heat to blistering. If hot was good, hotter was better. Lizzie had scorched her butt one day, sneaking in a dip with friends and the hot tub was gone a day later—legal reasons, his mother had stated.

She was a lawyer, she'd know.

"There's some lemon tofu pie in the bottom drawer. It's crustless but you'd never know it." She gestured with her head and picked up her briefcase, never happy when anything cluttered her kitchen counter, not even her own stuff. "I'm going to change then I'll be down to make dinner. What is that smell?" She walked and sniffed until her nose led her to Cort. "Have you showered today?"

"Of course, Mom."

"Is this some new cologne you're trying? The latest thing?"

"I—no. It's not."

She looked him up and down before turning with her briefcase. Taking off her high heels, she carried them in her other hand and she headed toward the door. "We'll get to the bottom of the way you smell later."

After she'd gone, Lizzie rolled her eyes. "I wonder what's for dinner? Tofu casserole?"

"We know tofu pie is for dessert," Cort mumbled.

"How long do you think she'll be on this one?" Lizzie joined him and the two of them stared blankly into the refrigerator.

"Let's go grab some burgers and fries," Cort whispered.

Cort shut his locker and looked down crowded senior hall for Rachel. Her dark hair was easy to spot, long and shimmery against her back. She was at her locker with her blond bomb friends, Ticia and Jennifer. The girls laughed. It wasn't a malicious laugh; Cort had never seen Rachel be the kind of girl that Bree, Megan and Shaylee had been that day in the salon. There was something different about Rachel, something that set her and her friends in an exclusivity that enticed.

He had yet to figure out his plan to show her he wasn't just another idiot jock with a great bod, better face and too much talent. The dance was coming up. Maybe he'd ask her and spend the night impressing her.

"Is it true?" The low whisper caused Cort to jump. One of his buddies, Eric, stood with Chad and Ben, his other friends. Eric's sky-blue eyes lit with mischief. His curly blonde hair looked like he'd forgotten to do anything but shake it out after his shower.

"Is what true?" Cort started down the hall toward Rachel and the girls and the guys followed.

"That you're working at that nail place?"

Cort couldn't keep his face from heating, but he kept his walk steady and cool. "Yeah, so?"

Eric pulled him to a stop. The guys stared at him. "Are you serious, man?"

"It was the only place I could find a job, dude." Cort started walking again, noticing that Rachel and Ticia were heading to class.

"But it's, like, a *nail* salon," Ben said.

"Yeah," Chad added. "Do they really do nails there?"

Cort snorted. "'Course they do nails."

The guys started laughing, elbowing each other and Cort instantly felt defensive and stopped. "What?"

After his laugh trickled, Eric said, "So what do you do? Take out the trash?"

"Sweep the floor?" Chad asked.

Ben stuck his elbow in Eric's ribs. "Clean windows?"

When the boys laughed again, Cort's face sizzled. He'd been so desperate for work, he hadn't thought about what everybody would think. He figured Bree, Megan and Shaylee and their big mouths had spread the word.

"Just forget it," he scowled, walking faster.

But the boys hung on him like a pack of wild dogs. He neared Rachel and Ticia and the noise the guys were making brought Rachel's curious eyes to his.

He stopped a distance away for damage control and faced

31

the group of laughing boys with a blooming snarl. "Cut it out."

"Dude, I can't believe you're doing grudge work in some nail salon," Eric said.

"It was all there was, now screw off."

"All right, all right." Eric backed away. "See you at lunch. You driving?"

Cort jerked his head in a yes and quickly turned. Couldn't they see he'd been left with no other options? Now he was on the freaking roaster for who knows how long while everybody fried him for it.

His quick glance told him he'd missed his chance to talk to Rachel – she was already gone. With another scowl, he continued to Economics.

Was it just his imagination or were people staring at him with a laugh in their eyes? He'd been stared at plenty. He was used to being admired, in fact. But this whispering mocking stuff was like acid on his skin.

I'm Cort Davies. He took the stairs up, two at a time. But rambling off his accomplishments and reminding himself of his social status did nothing to erase the bitter taste damaged pride left in his mouth.

At lunch he drove the guys to the current spot where anybody who was anybody who wanted to be seen hung out. Kids streamed into Wendy's, cloistered around parked cars in the parking lot, watching who came and went.

He looked for Rachel's sleek black BMW.

"So, what's it like?" Eric asked as they parked, got out and scanned the lot for babes.

"What?" Cort found her perfect baby Beemer – parked all by itself. *Yeah, she's here.* He strode toward the restaurant with the guys behind him.

"That nail job—Chihuahua's."

"It's Chachi's," Cort corrected.

"Bree said you actually *did* her nails." Ben pushed the door open.

"That's what I do—nails."

"No freaking way." The news stopped Eric in the doorway, clogging the flow of bodies into the place.

"It's no biggie." Cort shouldered past, forcing himself not to feel those greasy feelings of humiliation again. "I made seventy-five dollars in two hours. That's more than you can say."

"Seriously?"

When Cort saw envy in his friend's eyes, he grinned, felt like himself again. "It's true." He pulled out the fifteen dollars in tips he'd gotten from the girls and rubbed it under his friend's noses. Then he confidently strode into the dining area and looked for Rachel.

She was surrounded by guys. His face drew tight. *Jeez, is that girl ever alone?* His buddies stood behind him, expounding in amazement at his earning power and good fortune landing such a high-paying job. But he didn't revel in the accolades. He was trying to figure out how to get to Rachel when she was always in the middle of a gang of guys.

Her light laughter pierced the noisy air and sent a tickle through his body he couldn't itch. He wanted to talk to her, had to catch her attention somehow. So he ordered, and kept casual glances aimed her way.

"Rache." Ticia elbowed her and the movement of her eyes toward another area of the dining room told Rachel to follow her gaze. She saw him—part boy, part man, all incredibly beautiful. Cort Davies stood in line with his friends.

She only glanced, knowing their eyes might meet. She'd not let on she enjoyed looking at him, not after his challenge to prove he wasn't just another jock. She doubted he was not, but she was willing to let him try to convince her.

He looked over and she granted him a smile, wondering how long it would take him to move into action.

He had his tray and gave her a nod as he moved to a table and sat. *Wouldn't he just die if I went over there?*

"So I picked up the CD, it's awesome," somebody was saying and she nodded, her attention diverted.

"Burn it for me, will you?" Rachel knew these guys would do anything for her and sure enough Todd agreed. "I'll see you later."

She stood, gave each of her friends a quick hug and slyly signaled to Ticia to follow. Why did approaching Cort cause butterflies to flock in her stomach? She had tons of guy friends, considered herself a connoisseur of guys in fact, but this guy—everything about him thrilled and terrified her.

She went to where he sat with Ben, Chad and Eric.

"What are you going to do?" Ticia whispered.

"Start something."

The look of utter surprise on Cort's face as he watched her approach made her tingle all over. "Hey," she stopped at his table.

"Hey." He was eating two cheeseburgers, a giant fry and a shake. "Wow," she said. "They not feeding you at home?"

He laughed and she did too, instantly easing the awkward tension. "Want some?" When he held out his shake, she couldn't resist and took a sip, then handed it back to him.

"So you're a gentleman. That's cool." It pleased her more than she let on.

"I want your number," Cort said and whipped out his cell phone.

She grinned. "That's private information I give only to close friends."

"I've known you since elementary school," Chad piped. "You can take my word for it, he's a good guy."

"We knew each other *in* elementary school," Rachel corrected nicely. "And I'll find out about him for myself."

"But I need to talk to you." Cort stood, looking into her eyes. "Where do you work?"

"You'll just have to find me." Rachel left him with a taunting smile and she and Ticia walked out in the noon sun and headed to her car.

"I wish I could do that." Ticia sighed as they got inside.

"You can do whatever you want, once you decide you want to do it." Rachel started her car with a smile and slipped on a pair of black sunglasses, looking at herself in her rear-view mirror. One point in Cort's column—he was a gentleman without pretense. Or he would have hesitated at sharing something their mouths would both touch.

She liked that.

In fact, she liked it a lot, and thought about what a nice

mouth he had—full, wide, tempting. She'd kissed guys, liked kissing enough. But nobody made her feel that fire inside she'd fantasized about since she'd first seen Ariel and Eric kiss and wondered if fireworks could explode as a result. Was Cort that kind of kisser? He had the right equipment, and she had no doubt he had experience. Intellectually, she understood kissing was not just about the physics behind it. In fact, after her lame experiences, she came to realize the emotional connection, who you were kissing, was far more important than technique.

It was a premeditated move not to share her phone number. She wanted to see the lengths he would go to reach her. She didn't mean to be easy, not in any sense of the word. Life was too full of exciting experiences not to make the most of it with a little sweat. Anyone with a brain knew working for something made the capture sweeter. Cort Davies would have to work hard if he wanted to capture her.

FOUR

The girl was insanely hot, Cort decided. The way she took his shake without any hesitation and wrapped those gorgeous lips around the straw had driven him nuts.

There was more of that enticing teasing in those blue cat eyes of hers too, when she refused to give him her phone number. If it was some kind of game he didn't care, if he played along, Rachel would make it totally fun.

He smiled at the flirting girls he passed in the hall at school. None of them mattered, not with Rachel at his fingertips.

"Cort!" He recognized the demanding voice and didn't acknowledge it. He was on his way to work and couldn't be late. "Hey!"

He shoved open the double doors, heading out into the afternoon sun.

"I need you to drop me off at home." Lizzie sounded both annoyed and out of breath when she finally was in stride with him.

"Can't." He opened the door of his white truck, got in. "I'm going to work."

She got in anyway. "You... found a job?" She exaggerated just to irritate him.

He revved the engine and waited for her to get out. She broke into a laugh.

"What's funny?" he asked.

"That any respectable place would hire a loser like you. Wait! It must not be respectable if they hired you."

"Get out."

"Seriously, I need a ride home."

"And seriously, I can't give you a ride now go bum one off one of your friends."

"You know none of my friends can drive yet."

"So hitch."

"Yeah, right."

"I'm going to be late, beat it."

She sat firmly, looking out the front window.

"Where do you work? No, let me guess. You pick up trash downtown for the city. Do you get to wear one of those ugly orange jumpsuits that make you look like you just escaped from prison?"

In one jerk, Cort leaned across her and thrust open the door, almost pushing her out. Then he saw Rachel coming through the parking lot with Ticia and Jennifer. He froze, sat back up and started to sweat.

It was no skin off his nose to scream and yell, occasionally even pound on his sister—in private. But both of them knew better than to attack in public. That kind of behavior might be a turn-off to Rachel who looked right at him.

He hoped the afternoon sun was blinding her, or the glare from his front windshield.

He got out, sent her casual nod. "Hey."

"Hey, Cort." Rachel looked at Liz and sent her a friendly wave. "Isn't that your sister?"

"Yeah. You know her?"

"We had PE together last term. Hi, Liz."

Cort's gut tightened when Liz rolled down the window and started talking.

"Rachel, what's up? Need a ride? Cort's giving them out today."

"I have my car."

"That's right, that cute black Beemer. How would it be?"

"It's great, actually."

"Well, Cort's going to pound me because I'm making him late for work. He has this mysterious job no one knows about."

"You mean the nail job?" Rachel asked, and smiled at Cort.

He wanted to dissolve into the asphalt. Instead, he dropped his head to his chest.

"Nail job?" Liz spit out, then started howling with laughter. Rachel, Ticia and Jennifer moved closer to the car, amused at Liz's extreme reaction.

"How did you know?" Cort asked Rachel, his voice quiet.

"It's the hot topic, Cort. Everybody knows. You're not embarrassed are you?"

Though his face was heating fast, he shook his head ignoring the sticky discomfort of the moment.

"'Course not. I make good money there."

"Make?" Lizzie interjected. "You've worked there, what, *a day*? No wonder you smell."

"Mean girl," Rachel said, still highly amused.

"I've been working there for two weeks." Cort's tone was sharp. Aimed at Lizzie it promised retribution.

"So were you advertising when you told me they did great nails at Miss Chachi's or being honest?" Rachel asked.

He crossed his heart. "Being honest."

Rachel looked at Ticia, at Jennifer, then back at Cort. "We go to La Nails in the mall but we'll give you a try." She started toward her car. "You've got a chance to impress me, Cort."

"I'll take that chance," he called after her. "Come this afternoon."

As she backed away, the breeze mussed her hair, stirring something deep inside of him. "When do you work?" she asked.

"Four to nine."

She lifted a shoulder demurely. "Maybe." Then she turned and he watched her hips swing to her car.

"Woohoo. You have it for her, don't you?" Lizzie asked, rolling up her window.

The buzz of seeing Rachel and talking to her covered the total frustration he felt at what Lizzie had said. "She's a cool girl and all."

"Heavy emphasis on the *and all.*" Liz snickered as they drove.

"Why don't you keep your mouth shut, anyway?"

"Ashamed of your new employment?"

"No."

"Then why the big secret?"

"How many guys do you know that do nails, Lizzie?"

"None. Well, one, now. But it's pretty cool, actually. Think of all the girls you'll meet. I should think that alone would be enough for you to shout about it."

She was right. It will be a haven of females if Chachi's is anything like the other nail salons he'd happened by. Always packed with women. In the two weeks he'd worked there the only business the place had seen was the three girls he knew.

He was shocked enough to stop in the doorway when he saw half a dozen girls from school in the salon, waiting, once he got there.

Miss Chachi and the girls were talking to them, and Miss Chachi lit up like a flashlight when he came in. Bustling over, she was all smiles.

"Cort here, Cort here. Yes. Here he is, girls. Cort." She grabbed his sleeve, pulled him down for a whisper that burned his ear. "You late. These girls been here since three-forty-five. They all ask for you. I can't have this again. You be here right after school, understand?"

He nodded, took off his jacket and smiled at the grinning girls. "Hey." They all greeted him and he said, "You know, Tiaki does a great manicure. And Misu and Jasmine are pros at pedicures. Check it out."

Two of the girls agreed and Miss Chachi was delighted.

"Who's first?" he asked. They all raised their hands. He kept himself from breaking into a flattered laugh.

As he worked, he got to know the girls who had been nothing more than smiling, flirty faces at school. He learned that Maria de Silva played a wicked violin. He'd seen her in the orchestra, had never forgotten the way her shiny hair swung when she passionately played her instrument. But he'd never met her.

Kristen Jones was on drill team. He saw her at the games, and knew her brother Paul. But he always thought she was kind of stuck up. He was surprised to find her totally nice.

Bree's other friend, Morgan was just as superficial and into the gossip scene as Bree, Shaylee and Megan. These girls all looked the same; like teenage Barbie's with their striped blonde hair worn French fry straight, light glossy lips and skin that looked like it spent too many hours in the tanning booth.

Time flew. He didn't have a chance to check his watch. Finally his last client left, a girl by the name of Sharon who promised to tell her mom and all of her friends about him. He was exhausted, his fingers ached and his nose was filled with enough powder residual that he finally let loose a violent sneeze.

He ran his hands through his hair and let out a sigh just as Rachel walked through the door. It was twenty minutes to nine and the other girls had been dismissed by Miss Chachi earlier.

"Welcome, welcome." Miss Chachi went directly to Rachel with her nod and smile.

"Is it too late?" Rachel asked, looking around for a clock.

"No, no. You are here for Cort, yes? For nails? Manicure? Pedicure? Massage?"

Rachel looked at Cort, coming to the front of the store. "He does all of that?"

"He do anything, yes. Cort do anything at all. You want,

he do." Miss Chachi's smiling eyes slid to his with a glint of something.

"Hey," Cort said, sticking his aching hands into his back pockets. As much as he wanted to spend time with Rachel, he hoped Miss Chachi wasn't going to make him do another set of nails.

"She want you," Miss Chachi said. The statement brought an awkward laugh from both Rachel and Cort.

"Sorry I'm late," Rachel began. "I had other obligations."

The mystery of her ate at him. She was conveniently vague, just enough to lure. "No problem, but I'm done for the night."

"You not done." Miss Chachi's smile flipped to a frown. "You can do one more set. Here." She took hold of his sleeve and dragged him back to his table but he pulled free.

"No," Rachel said, seeing the struggle of wills. "I'll come back."

"It's late," Cort told Miss Chachi as respectfully as he could. "And I have school tomorrow."

He strode back, gathered his coat and returned to her. Something ominous simmered behind her black eyes. He didn't like it.

He looked at Rachel. "I'll walk you out. See you tomorrow, Miss Chachi."

Then he held the salon door open for Rachel and as she passed, he smelled the great shampoo she used. Maybe it was just that his nostrils had been assaulted all day by acetone and nail junk but he took in a long, deep breath and sighed.

"Your employer reminds me of Mrs. Meers."

"Yeah, she does."

"You've seen *Thoroughly Modern Millie?*" Another point for Cort Davies, Rachel thought, a guy with some culture.

"In New York," he said.

She could relate to a guy who had traveled like she had. "I liked it."

"It was pretty cool, yeah."

Although her car was parked next to his white truck neither stopped. They continued to walk the emptiness of Main Street at a slow and easy pace. Inviting, cozy, the street was lined with buildings from the turn of the century, each painted a different, soft shade that, under the moon's hazy light, looked ghostly now. Most businesses were closed, but their windows were lined with colored lights. Cort and Rachel peered in the various store-front windows as they passed.

"You like New York?" Rachel asked. For her, how a person viewed New York was telling. New York was a pivotal place, where fresh ideas sprung, where anything was possible. Someone who couldn't appreciate that was not someone she would spend much time with.

He shrugged. "It's a cool place—kind of crowded."

Rachel's heart took a hit. She tried to ignore it. "But you can learn a lot watching crowds."

"I guess."

They passed Minerva's, a little imported gourmet foods shop. The rich scent of coffee snuck out in the air and they stopped under the purple and green awning and looked at the display of Harry Potter chocolates in the window.

"Smells good," Rachel said. "I love the smell of coffee."

"Want some?" he asked.

"Sure."

He opened the door for her and they went in. The store was warm inside; the cozy air filled with the mix of brewing coffee, chocolate and cinnamon. The petite woman behind the counter greeted them with a grin that deepened a smattering of wrinkles. "What can I get you?"

Cort looked at Rachel, waited for her to give her order. "I'll take a medium coffee with cream and sugar."

"Make that two," Cort said.

They browsed the store, enjoying the odd English biscuit, the beautifully boxed Belgian chocolates. Finally they sat at a small, green wrought-iron table in the center of the large front window where the Harry Potter candy was on display.

"You work at Chachi's, don't you?" the woman asked Cort as she set down their steaming white mugs.

"Yeah, I do."

"I've seen you go in. How's it doing? Business can be kind of slow in this part of town."

"It's picking up." Cort thought of how he'd increased Miss Chachi's revenue. He glanced at her nails. "You should come in."

The woman laughed heartily with a look at her hands. "Not when I use my hands as much as I do, there's no point."

"We do pedicures and stuff too." Nervously, he picked up his hot mug and sipped. He couldn't believe he was talking about nail stuff.

"Sounds good. I'm Minerva by the way."

"Cort. And this is Rachel."

"Nice to meet you. Maybe I'll drag by aching feet down there one day and let you give me a pedicure."

"Any time. Great coffee," he smiled at her.

"You two have a good night." Minerva went about tending the store.

Rachel sat back with her coffee studying him.

"What?" he finally asked.

She hesitated before she said, "Nothing." But a guy who could handle himself with adults, she liked. A guy who would even consider rubbing some strange woman's corny feet and scraping away yucky calluses was definitely impressive, whether he thought intellectually about New York or not.

"I won't sleep now." Cort rubbed his hands down his face.

"Why? The caffeine?"

He nodded, rubbing his knuckle joints.

"Me too," she said. "I should have had hot chocolate. But I love coffee. What do you do when you can't sleep?"

He shrugged. "Get on the computer, read. If I'm really wired, I work out."

"Like what?"

"Weights and stuff."

That would account for his ripped bod, she thought, skimming her gaze nonchalantly down the length of him as she took another drink. "I check things out on the internet."

"You on Facebook?" he asked.

"Yeah."

Drawing his lower lip between his teeth, Cort studied her. She was so mysterious. He'd figured this little encounter would enlighten him but all he knew about her was that she loved coffee, sometimes suffered with insomnia and liked to surf the internet in the late hours of night. "What do you look for?" he asked.

"Anything and everything. There are so many places I want to go, things I want to see and understand. It's a tool, you know? A kind of computerized binocular."

"Watching people?" he suggested.

"Not like that, no." But something alluring colored her eyes.

He leaned forward. "I want your phone number."

Her hand clasped her purse, opened it. Pulling out her vibrating cell phone, she smiled. He didn't know why the motion made him jealous, but it did. Somebody was calling her, some guy no doubt.

"Just a second." She stood, turning her back to him. He stared at her long, silky hair hanging down her back.

"Hey." Her tone was altogether too pleased to be speaking to whomever she was addressing. He sat back, eyes firmly on her every move. "No, I was too late…yeah, I know." She laughed and the sound made him antsy. "I'm going to be a few minutes longer. Having coffee. Yeah. Okay, see you then. Bye." She clicked off the phone and turned around, facing him.

"Well."

Taking the cue, he stood, and left some change for a tip. "Yeah, I gotta get going too." He walked with her to their cars. Lights were still on in the salon. He saw Miss Chachi talking heatedly into the phone at the front desk.

He stayed in the dark where the street lights didn't reach,

next to Rachel's car door. As she dug through her purse for keys, the moon, barely a slice of light in the black sky, lit her skin to cream.

She glanced in the salon window. "Looks like Mrs. Meers is plotting."

Cort nodded. The little woman pounded her fist on the counter as she spoke into the phone.

"She's…yeah." He better keep his mouth shut, Cort decided. Gossiping was not his style.

Rachel opened her car and Cort smelled leather. Money.

She sat inside and looked up at him. "Thanks for the coffee." When she started the engine it purred. "Facebook me," she told him with a smile, then shut the door.

Cort couldn't sleep so he stared at his computer screen, at the Facebook home page. His fingers itched to type in her name address since she still hadn't given him her cell phone number. Of course he could look it up in the school phone book, but nobody did that. If they did, they never called without getting a green light first.

Was her Facebook friend invitation a yellow light?

His fingers touched the keys just as his bedroom door opened and his mother walked in after one knock.

"Cort." She stayed in the door, knowing how he valued his privacy. "Sorry I got home so late."

"It's okay." He turned, leaning casually back on the computer desk. "What's up?"

She'd changed into her pajamas, her reading glasses propped low on her nose and she held a stack of papers in her arms.

"Just going over some files. You and Liz find that Tofu quiche I left in the fridge?"

"I wasn't here for dinner. I was at work."

She shifted, smiling. "Liz mentioned you found a job. But she won't tell me where, said that needed to come from you."

"It's nothing, just a service job."

"What kind of service?"

"Uh, maintenance." For some reason he couldn't explain, he couldn't tell his mother he was working at Chachi's nail salon. But he couldn't lie to her either. He figured truth, even in a roundabout form, was better than a lie.

"Maintenance? Well, work is work. I'm just glad you finally found something. Now remember what we set up: ten percent goes to charity, twenty-five to your savings account and thirty to your college fund. The rest is yours to do what you want with. How much are you making, anyway?"

"Minimum." Plus tips, he thought, and those would add up nicely.

"Well, that's better than nothing." She turned, ready to leave him alone. "Don't be up too late. Take a melatonin if you need some help falling asleep. It's natural. 'Night."

"'Night." Something about tonight, seeing Miss Chachi vehemently talking into the phone, stuck with him and he couldn't figure out why.

Turning his thoughts to something less confusing, he went for it and typed in Rachel's name, waiting for her to accept his friend request. It seemed to take forever. Finally, the IM window popped up. His stomach fluttered.

RACHEL: yes, we can IM. Cool

CORT: can't sleep, like i figured. you? what are you looking at?

RACHEL: stuff

He rubbed his face with both hands, letting out a groan. Was she purposefully evasive? She drove him deliciously crazy.

RACHEL: i could spend hours just looking at the live web cams of times square. The streaming video is awesome. Here's the link. Turn up your volume and you can hear horns honking. It's the coolest, hits me like a drug

Cort found the website but kept the instant messaging box open in the lower left corner of his screen. He turned up the volume. Sure enough, people and cars cruised at two a.m. in downtown Manhattan. The far-off sound of life bustling was exciting.

RACHEL: cool, right?

At that moment, with his insomnia, it was great to open the front door and step out into a stream of life, rather than the stillness of a town like Pleasant View. He could walk with millions of others unable to sleep, and not feel alone.

CORT: it's awesome, especially tonight

RACHEL: but then we wouldn't be here

CORT: what if we were there?

RACHEL: then i'd show you my favorite places, like the borders that stays open all night on 79ᵗʰ we could drown ourselves in lattes and books.

CORT: how about we go find the web cams? climb the buildings and stuff?

Rachel laughed out loud. Wasn't he full of surprises? She

expected him to be online tonight. She expected him to try to get her. What she hadn't expected was how much she'd enjoy this little back and forth messaging.

She'd been checking out options for housing at NYU, her college of choice, when the friend request box had popped onto the screen from Facebook.

RACHEL: fancy yourself spideyman, do you?

CORT: doesn't every guy? what about you? got a complex?

RACHEL: no. i don't see myself in a tight suit jumping around buildings. i'd rather take the subway

CORT: you'd be a limo girl

RACHEL: that's how much you still don't know about me

CORT: that's going to change

A pleasant shudder streamed through Rachel. He was just aggressive enough to be interesting and not be a turn-off.

RACHEL: i'll expect good things then. later, Cort

CORT: bye, Rache

Then Cort had the sinking feeling he'd made a huge mistake by calling her Rache instead of Rachel. It was something he did, nicknaming friends. Was she mad? Had anyone else ever called her Rache?

"Crud." He'd feel that out later, if he hadn't cracked the delicate steps he'd already taken to get to her.

When the instant message box closed, he stared at the live video stream of New York City alive and thriving, lights gleaming and pulsing. In the hum of distant sound he heard brakes screeching, horns honking. Music. He smiled.

FIVE

Cort didn't smell the toxic fumes of acetone and nail product anymore when he was at Miss Chachi's and was glad for it. He didn't want to think what that meant—that his nose or brain or both were being eaten away by the caustic stuff.

He needed the money, so he ignored the hazards.

He'd made a hundred and seventy-five dollars in tips the first week, and brought Miss Chachi and her girls dozens of clients who spread the word to their mothers. Now, the place wasn't empty anymore when he reported to work in the afternoon.

He planned to ask Rachel to the dance Friday night, hoped she would come in for a nail fill but she didn't. He'd not been able to corner her at school, surrounded as she always was by her posse.

He worked, and kept glancing toward the door, hoping to see her. But everybody except her seemed to need their nails done for the dance.

He'd never ask her any other way but in person. Of course she might have already been asked, all the hot girls had been this close to deadline. Even if she had, he wanted her to know he wanted to go with her.

He was filling Bree's nails, wondering why she was there

again. She hadn't had any noticeable outgrowth. Megan and Shaylee were there as well, both having their toes painted coordinating colors to match their dresses for the dance.

"He's going to die when he sees it," Bree said, clacking on a piece of gum. "It's the prettiest dress ever."

Megan nodded from her perch in the pedicure chair. "For sure. I wish I'd seen it first."

"You wouldn't look good in the color anyway," Bree said.

"You're not the only one who can wear white."

"It fits me," Bree said.

"Yeah right," Shaylee snickered. "Red would be more like it."

"Shut up." Bree watched Cort paint the sparkly pink nail polish on her nails. "So, you going, Cortie?"

"Not yet."

The girls exchanged sly glances of disbelief. "I'd ditch my date if you want," Megan told him.

"Get in line, ho," Shaylee shot before softening her tone for Cort. "How come? Who are you going to ask?"

After hearing the way they talked, knowing the way they spread things, Cort only shrugged. Again the girls looked at each other.

"Who is she? Come on, you can tell us."

And it'll be all over the place like regurgitated food. Not to mention what they might say about Rachel. Still, he was curious what girls thought of her. Most of the guys he knew saw Rachel as this elite, untouchable idol.

"Do you know Rachel Baxter?" he asked. He kept his eyes on Bree's nails, so as to not appear too interested.

Bree tugged her hand and brought his eyes to hers. "Is that who you want to ask?"

"What do you know about her?"

"First tell me if she's the one you want to ask."

"Yeah, tell us," Megan piped.

Bree pulled her hand away from him. "Answer me, Cort."

"I did answer you." He snatched her hand back and started painting again. "Hold still or it will wreck."

"You did not. You were annoyingly vague," Bree snapped. "But two can play that game." She didn't say anything more, just clacked on her gum.

"I'm not playing any game." Cort was frustrated. Why couldn't these girls be real?

"Right." Bree hissed out a laugh. "I've seen you in action. You play just like the rest of us."

Shame heated his face and kept his eyes on her nails as he brushed the final coat of pink. Is that what everybody thought? He wanted to smear the plastic-pink nail polish he'd painstakingly applied and kick her out the door but his wallet depended on the job.

"You're done," he told her with bite in his tone.

Bree surveyed her nails critically then slid him a snotty glare, her gum clacking like a gun-shot. "I guess they'll do." She stood. "Oops. I forgot to get your tip out of my purse and my nails are wet. Guess you'll have to wait till next time."

Shaylee and Megan exchanged looks of shock. Shaylee whispered, "Way harsh, Bree."

Frustrated, Cort felt his jaw start to ache as he worked to keep from yelling at her. He stood. "Look. I'm sorry if I pissed you off."

Miss Chachi was suddenly there, like a hound dog on the scent of something. "Everything all right?" she asked.

"Just trying to decide if I like this fill or not." Bree held her hands up, fingers spread for Miss Chachi to examine.

"Bree—" The last thing Cort needed was Miss Chachi's disapproval.

Miss Chachi took Bree's hands and examined them. "If you not satisfied, he do it again."

Cort glanced at the clock, then at the waiting area where a half-dozen more girls sat, waiting. If he'd been an octopus he couldn't have finished all of their nails. He began to sweat.

"No." Bree tilted her head, hair swinging like a pendulum. "I think they're fine, thanks."

With that, Miss Chachi went back to the front desk.

Bree leaned into Cort. "I just saved your butt." She pushed her hip, with her purse dangling next to it, his direction. "Now get me my wallet."

Cort rolled his eyes before digging into her purse. He'd never seen so much junk; lipsticks, compacts, perfume and— jeez, a tampon. Finally he found the raspberry wallet with bright cherries and Juicy written all over it.

"Hmm." Bree tapped her finger to her chin in thought. Cort started to burn.

"Forget it," he said and turned.

Quickly, Bree shoved a ten dollar bill in his hand. "Your customer relations needs some work." She waited at the front of the salon while Shaylee and Megan's pedicures finished up.

Cort didn't look at her when she gossiped with the other

girls waiting. He could only wonder what Bree was telling them. And the snarling looks he got from Miss Chachi bothered him.

Before he took his next client, he strode to the front of the salon. The girls quieted. Bree tilted her head with a smile meant to be mean.

Cort ignored her. "I know most of you are waiting for me but," he smiled in the way he knew most girls responded to, big and with his eyes wide. "I only have two hands. I think you'll find Misu, Tiaki, Jasmine and Abby are great at this. Give them a try. Seriously."

Some of the girls checked their watches and reluctantly sat at Tiaki, Jasmine and Misu's tables.

Cort hoped the effort would go a ways in appeasing Miss Chachi and proving to witchy Bree he controlled girls better than she did.

Bree waved her newly done nails Cort's direction as she got ready to leave the salon. "Bye Cortie."

* * *

By the end of the night, Cort had filled seven sets of nails.

He rubbed his fingers, glanced at the clock on the wall— a photo of some place in Vietnam, he presumed, with its lush hills and muddy waters, set in a clock face. Nine o'clock and Rachel still had not come in.

The other girls cleaned their work stations and Miss Chachi counted money at the front desk, looking over at him every now and then.

He straightened his table, turned off the bright work light and stretched as he went to the front. "Wow," he started in an effort to be friendly. "What a day, huh?"

Miss Chachi closed the register. Her dark eyes pinned him. "We still not make enough for me to pay rent. If more customer don't come, I take tips to pay."

"What?"

"You heard me. If I can't pay, there no job. No job, you no money."

"But what about the girls I've brought in?"

She nodded. "Very good, yes. But not enough. We need more. This place cost money to run. I have overhead."

"Maybe it's that you're in over your head," he muttered.

She came around to the front of the desk. "You a nice boy, Cort. You work hard. You want to keep job, yes?"

"Yeah."

She patted his arm but her hand was icy. "See? We need each other."

"I'm doing what I can," he said, exasperated.

"You can do more. Now." She went to the schedule and pulled it out, laying it in front of him on the counter. "Tomorrow I need you until close."

"What? I can't. I have a dance tomorrow night. In fact, I won't be here at all tomorrow."

Her black brows hardened. "That not possible. You have eleven appointments."

"Tiaki and Misu and the girls can take them."

"They come for you." She pounded her fist on the

schedule and he jumped. The girls stared for a moment, before going back to cleaning as if they had seen nothing.

Cort was speechless. Something in his gut didn't feel right. Miss Chachi's hard face softened. She laid her icy hand on his arm. "We work something out. You come in for a little while, eh?"

Drawing his lower lip between his teeth, he stared at her, trying to figure her out. She was hot, then cold. He didn't want either extreme. "Uh, sure. Okay."

"See you tomorrow. You go home. Rest your hands." She took them in hers, studying them. She shook her head with a tsk-tsk. "Soak in warm water and peanut oil with a little fresh ginger. Then they feel better."

He didn't have any peanut oil or fresh ginger, though he considered that his mother may have some on hand—with her weird new eating jag.

At home, he went to his computer instead of soaking his fingers.

He wanted Rachel.

It was insultingly late now to ask a girl to a dance, no respectable guy did that—or they looked like a loser. He hoped she'd come online so he could fish for whether or not anybody else had asked her. Maybe he could explain why he hadn't—because he hadn't been able to. Maybe she wouldn't think he was just scrounging for a last minute date, like it looked.

When she didn't respond and the little box indicated that she was "off line", he sighed. Maybe he'd be working all night at Miss Chachi's after all.

SIX

Countryside Manor used to give her the shivers with its funky smell of stale air, body oil, medicine and cafeteria food and howling voices echoing down empty halls. Rachel forced herself not to let those things keep her from doing what she had to do.

People depended on her.

Countryside Manor looked like a poor man's Tara from Gone with the Wind, with white columns and black shutters set against vinyl clapboard siding—falsely inviting when its occupants would move in and never move out.

The air was always stuffy inside and Rachel quickly took off her black coat, gloves and scrappy scarf, hanging them on a brass peg near the front desk. She smiled at Charity, the elderly receptionist with a grey beehive of hair.

"They're waiting for you." Charity nodded toward the gathering room.

"Great. Thanks."

"Mr. Fowler's in a foul mood. Ignore him."

Rachel knew better than to let the old man get under her skin. She passed rooms with open doors and didn't glance inside—it hurt seeing those stuck in their beds from neglect or whatever reason.

Magic Hands • Jennifer Laurens

She'd been coming to Countryside for months, reading passages from plays to the older people who called the rest home, home. It helped her feel like she was making a contribution somehow, and helped her learn to change her voice and fine-tune her acting talent.

Her interest in acting was pricked after she saw Jennifer bravely take on roles in junior high. This reading on the side was her own little secret, and until she felt ready to let the world in on it, it would remain just that.

There were seven gathered tonight; some in wheelchairs, others propped on couches and chairs scattered in the room. They all perked up when she entered. The sight warmed her heart and brought a smile to her face.

"Hey." She laughed when some of the old guys pulled her down for a kiss on the cheek.

"Here's our girl." With a twinkle in her eye, Mannie was always happy to see her. The older woman patted Rachel's hand. "What are you going to read to us tonight, lovey?"

Rachel pulled a seat up close to the little semicircle, since hearing was an issue for most of them. "Hamlet."

"Oh," gushed Lily, her frail hands clasped to her chest. "One of my favorites."

Martin Fowler scowled. "Blitsy, I say."

"Want me to wheel you over to the window so you can look out at the deer?" Rachel asked him before she began reading.

"Hell no. A blitsy love story is better than watching a herd of dull deer any day."

"I'd hardly call Hamlet a love story, Martin." Mannie

shook her head. "It's a tragedy."

"Aren't they all love stories?" Martin shot.

"See?" Lily nodded. "You do like our girl."

"Well of course I like her," Martin scoffed. "I just don't agree with her choice of reading material."

"Well she's not going to come in here and read an old war book, not when you're out numbered five to one, Martin." Mannie pointed her finger at him.

"Why not?" Martin asked. "Spies and bombs would be a helluva lot more entertaining than dancing and romance. Or Shakespeare. Maybe I will go over to the window after all." In a burst of pride, he tried to wheel himself away from the wide-eyed gathering, but his feeble body was too weak.

Rachel pushed him to the window. She tried not to smile. Little bickerings were common between Martin and Mannie. She often wondered if the two old people really liked each other and were just juvenile about their feelings.

"Anytime you want me to come get you," Rachel whispered to him, "raise your hand or wave."

"I'll do neither tonight!" Martin turned away from her.

Rachel joined the others. The eager faces of the women touched her heart. She opened the script, one of many she collected, and started reading.

As usual, she threw herself into the story and the characters, playing each role with such enthusiasm she lost track of time. When she finished, she blushed at the soft applause that followed.

"Is there anybody special in your life, lovey?" Mannie asked.

Magic Hands • Jennifer Laurens

"Heavens yes." Lily leaned forward with effort. "She's so beautiful. There are many young men in love with her."

Rachel's cheeks heated. "Nobody's in love with me, Lily."

"Why not?" Agatha asked. Usually she said nothing, her oxygen tube the only hum Rachel ever heard from the woman. "What's wrong with them?"

"I should say," Mannie protested. "They need their eyes examined is what's wrong with them."

"I have lots of guy friends," Rachel said.

"So you say," Mannie piped. "But a girl as pretty as you should have young men knocking down her door."

Lily nodded her little head. "In my day, I had fifteen suitors at one time. Good-looking fellows at that."

"I'm sure." Rachel couldn't keep the smile from her face. The fervor these ladies felt for her social life was hilarious. "But I'm not interested in getting serious."

"And why not?" With great effort, Martin had made it half-way across the floor to them. Rachel wheeled him back to the little circle.

"Because—"

"Mannie's right," Martin scoffed. "You should find a fella and settle down."

Rachel laughed. "I'm only seventeen."

"I was engaged at your age," Lily's soft voice was light and dreamy. "Met my Henry when those packs of young men were coming around. He was one of them."

"See?" Martin boomed.

"But girls don't get married that young anymore," Rachel protested good-naturedly.

"That's the problem with society." Mannie was getting worked up, Rachel could tell by the way her face reddened. "If young people found their companions and settled down, there would be less trouble, I know it."

"Nonsense." Martin waved disagreeably at her. "Marriage has everything to do with trouble."

"I was wonderfully happy with my Henry for seventy years," Lily said. Rachel's heart ached for the little woman whose eyes misted now.

"Guys." She didn't want the discussion getting out of hand. "I'm not going to get married any time soon. I have to graduate, go to college."

"Well at least find yourself somebody to be arm-in-arm with, lovey," Mannie said. "Bring him round to meet us, will you?"

Lily nodded. "Oh, how lovely to meet him. What did you say his name was?"

Rachel laughed. "I didn't say." She stood and kissed each one on their soft cheeks. Martin grabbed her arm and kept his shaking hand on it as he pulled her down for a whisper.

"You don't listen to those old dames. You take your time but don't wait too long or you'll end up like me."

Martin had never married. He often complained about it, along with everything else he complained about. But Rachel sensed the deep regret behind those complaints.

"Next week bring us the Dirty Dozen," he told her, loud enough so the women would holler at him. They did.

Rachel walked to her car with a smile but inside she carried a dull, familiar ache. It was always like this when she left Countryside—joy mixed with sorrow. She never left without thinking about life, love, and choices.

When she had her first serious crush, she was devastated that the boy had been childishly cruel and ignored her. It hurt her young heart so much she swore she would never be serious about another boy until she was millions of miles away from Pleasant View and in her late twenties at the very least.

The commitment was extreme, and kept her home a lot of weekends because she refused to go on single dates—choosing instead to hang with friends in groups. She couldn't believe she'd made it to her senior year without going to a dance or a prom or anything else like it.

It wasn't for lack of friends or invitations. All of her friends were guys and all of them at one time or another had asked her out. But she preferred hanging in a casual group. That way, things never got too deep. Her feelings stayed intact. She was afraid of getting hurt, a secret she only admitted to herself.

She thought of Cort as she drove by the now-dark Chachi's. Something about him was different than her other guy friends. Probably the part of her that was guy-starved imagined Cort was different—because she wanted him to be.

She pulled into her driveway. *You're doing it again, setting yourself up.* This same kind of irrational emotional thinking had made her think her first crush was different—and he hadn't been.

But then they'd only been in sixth grade.

The house was dark, her parents had gone to bed and the usual note was stuck to the fridge for her.

*Rache-Dad flies out tomorrow so we went to bed early. Some
boy named Cort came by for you around nine-fifteen. What
a cutie. Is this someone I should know about? We'll talk over
breakfast.*

Love, Mom

Cort Davies was going for *her*. Rachel smiled, enjoying
a delicious fluttering deep inside. Maybe she'd let the feeling
stay a little tonight, it felt so good and completely dissolved
any of the sad feelings she often carried for hours after being
at Countryside.

She grabbed a yogurt, set the house alarm and went
up to her bedroom. The house was quiet, the way she was
accustomed to, when the thumping sounds of their five cats at
play was the only sound that bounced off the walls.

She went right to her computer and got on Facebook.
One of the guys from her group of friends had messaged her
and she clicked on it, disappointed the message wasn't from
Cort.

TOD: *Rache, Just wanted to ask again – for the dance
tomorrow night. Come on, can't you, just this once? For me?*

For a second, Rachel let herself think about what she
would do if the invite was from Cort. Going to a dance with
Cort Davies would definitely start a rumble of gossip. Being
seen with him would launch her into a stratosphere she wasn't
sure she wanted to orbit in.

She'd never strove for popularity, always the center of

attention in her own comfortable way, and that worked for her. But no teenage girl could deny how excellent it would be to be seen with a guy like Cort.

But a guy *like* Cort wasn't who she'd be seen with. She let the brief fantasy of the two of them continue in her mind. Cort is who she'd be seen with. He was the top of the social ladder at Pleasant View.

She dipped into her yogurt then typed a reply to Todd.

sorry, toddy. can't. you know how i am.

Sitting back, yogurt in hand, Rachel stared at the screen knowing full well that if Cort was asking, she'd be tempted to say yes. As cute as Cort was, as interesting as it was to watch him make moves for her, she'd have to do just as she did with any other guys—refuse. That was the only way not to have her heart derailed.

The instant message popped onto the screen and that warm fluttering in her belly returned.

CORT: hey.

RACHEL: heard you came by

CORT: wanted to ask you something but it's too late now

RACHEL: hmm. going to tell me or keep me in the dark?

CORT: doesn't matter now. your mom's nice. i didn't know your dad was an airline pilot. no wonder you get around

RACHEL: i'll take it you meant geographically. yeah,

we've always traveled. nice perk

CORT: lucky you. the rest of us have to earn it

RACHEL: hey, wait a minute. my dad's gone half the month. we earn it, believe me

CORT: O man Sorry

Cort stopped, waiting to see if she was mad. That was the last thing he wanted to do—make her mad at him. After a long pause, she replied:

RACHEL: you still there?

CORT: i didn't mean anything by it. sorry

A guy who could apologize. Rachel liked that. Another point for Cort. Now, he'd pricked her interest asking her something and then not asking her. She had to know what it was.

RACHEL: i'll forget it if you tell me why you came by

CORT: it's too late. there's no point

Truthfully, Cort was afraid if he told her and she didn't like the idea of going to the dance with him, she'd be turned off before he had a chance to prove himself.

CORT: you going to the dance tomorrow night?

RACHEL: was that it?

CORT: no

Rachel chewed on the spoon in her mouth, disappointed.

RACHEL: no, I'm not going

CORT: me either. i have to work

Rachel felt a rush of relief. He wasn't going with anyone—good. She decided to let down her guard just a little.

RACHEL: so i can come in and get my nails done then?

Hadn't he been waiting for that for all week now? He'd

count the hours until tomorrow.

CORT: i'll be there, if that's what you mean

RACHEL: so, what happened?

CORT: what do you mean?

RACHEL: i didn't think you ever missed a dance.

CORT: this will be the first but, hey, it's cool. i'll get to spend the night with you

Rachel's spine tingled. He was dangling himself as bait. No wonder he was so hot. If she could, she'd reach through the computer and… After that, well, she wasn't sure what she'd do but she was pretty sure it would include wrapping her arms around him.

RACHEL: you have a way with words

CORT: just telling it like it is. so, where were you tonight your mom said you were at work. i didn't think you worked

Rachel set aside her spoon, tried not to feel irritated that he thought she was some rich, spoiled girl who didn't do anything but live off of her parents' money.

RACHEL: i have to go now

Cort's pulse skipped. He'd screwed up.

CORT: did i say something?

RACHEL: you said enough

CORT: let me say i'm sorry again. will that help?

RACHEL: maybe

CORT: i didn't mean anything by the not working comment. ok, i'll admit, i heard you were rich. i saw your house tonight, and you drive the beemer can you blame me?

RACHEL: no, and i can't expect you to be different than anybody else, either. see you later, Cort.

CORT: rache, wait

Cort waited for her to respond, his fingers tapping on the desk. He couldn't believe he'd blown it. In two seconds he'd blown it. Would she leave it at that? He typed again, desperate.

CORT: rache? if i had your phone number, we could talk. i could – i don't know, say i'm sorry again, kiss your feet, wash your car – something.

Cort ran his hands down his face and let out a sigh, staring at his own words on the screen.

RACHEL: you'd wash my car?

CORT: right now.

RACHEL: you'd kiss my feet?

CORT: i'd kiss wherever

Rachel shuddered thinking about it.

RACHEL: i'm not going to touch that. i'll see you tomorrow at school

CORT: what about your nails?

RACHEL: my nails need to be done so i'll see you at Miss Chachi's around seven

Cort sat back on a groan. She played him like a yo-yo, and it drove him lusciously crazy. He'd never sleep now, not with her surging through his veins.

He fell onto his bed and stared up at the ceiling where a poster of Sundance ski resort was tacked. He'd stuck the poster there years ago; found that dreaming about the slopes helped relax him on nights like this. But that was before he knew about girls. About how girls could keep his blood in a whirl that nothing could slow.

He wanted to talk to Rachel on the phone, hear that low, bass and guitar voice of hers. He wanted tomorrow to be here. He had a long night ahead of him, an even longer day with work. Until then, the poster wouldn't be enough.

He got up, sat down in front of his computer and clicked onto favorites. From there, he was one click away from the New York City web cam.

SEVEN

Rachel walked down the crowded hall with Ticia and Jennifer. The guys were at her elbows and heels, and she tried not to lose her patience.

Sam, a drummer for the school jazz band shook his head at Todd. "Forget it, dude. She's not interested in you because she's waiting for me to ask her." He nudged into her playfully.

"Right." Rachel rolled her eyes. Miss Tingey's class was mercifully near. "See you guys later."

"You driving for lunch?" Todd asked.

"How about that new place, Kippers Fish and Chips?" Pete asked, slowly trailing a rejected Todd across the hall to another classroom.

Rachel shrugged. "Maybe." She wanted to keep her options open.

With the boys gone, Jennifer leaned over. "Todd's driving you nuts, I can tell."

"When will he get the message?" Rachel stood outside Miss Tingey's door as other students entered.

"Never." Ticia strained a look down the hall. Her face broke into a big smile and Rachel turned. "He's so hot."

Cort and Chad came toward them. "They're both hot,"

71

Rachel murmured. "Carmel's looking good today."

"Uh-huh." Ticia agreed. Chad's code name was Caramel because he was the smoothest talking guy they'd ever overheard.

They had yet to come up with a code name for Cort, though they'd named all of his friends. As the boys approached, Rachel held the door for them and waved a goodbye to Jennifer and Ticia who went on to class.

Cort and Chad stopped, and Cort lifted his arm to hold the door open for her. The muscle in his bicep shifted and when his shirt lifted, Rachel caught a glimpse of low belly, lean and ripped. "After you," he said with a grin that sent a tingle through her.

Cort followed Rachel inside. She was amazingly aware of his presence behind her. She sat, watched as he greeted friends with the typical male greeting of knocking knuckles and slapping palms.

He looked over with a private nod, this greeting sexier. His dark eyes glittered with something secret.

Miss Tingey spoke, breaking their tight gaze. "Today's journal topic is *what is real*. I know this sounds ambiguous and I want it to. I want to hear what's real to you at this very moment. Today. Right now. Write."

The class started writing and Rachel thought about the topic. What was real for her was the flock of birds swarming inside of her for Cort. Real was the way he looked at her, with a look that said I want you. Real at that very moment was that she was dangerously close to abandoning her resolve to keep her heart protected.

What was real to Cort? She wondered.

Rachel looked amazing today in jeans and a light pink hoodie with Sweetstuff across the front of it. Yeah, she was pretty sweet, that was for sure. That was real. Cort tried not to let his eyes wander to where she sat. Real is this need I have to get to know her. So consuming. Like hunger.

"Anybody want to share?" Miss Tingey scanned the class for volunteers. No one raised their hands, the room unusually quiet. She smiled. "This one's more personal isn't it?" Slowly she paced in front of the room with her arms folded. "Why is it more personal?"

Somebody spoke. "Because it's where our brains are and that can incriminate."

Everyone laughed and Miss Tingey nodded. "True, but that's also what's interesting—to see where everybody's at this very moment. Who's brave? Or do I just call on people?"

"We could say whatever," one boy called out, "and you wouldn't know whether it was real or not."

"But that wouldn't be any fun," she teased.

"Real for me right now is keeping the friggin' deer out of my mom's yard," Kevin sighed.

Everyone laughed. Cort leaned over to him. "You still on that?"

Kevin slumped down in his chair. "Nothing works, man."

A general discussion about being honest or not followed. Finally Miss Tingey called on Maria de Silva.

Maria's cheeks flushed red. "Real right now is tonight's dance and I didn't get asked."

"I'll take you," a boy told her from the back. She looked

at him and turned even redder.

"Thank you, Maria." Miss Tingey scanned the room. "How about you, Cort?"

Cort shifted under the glare of the spotlight. He lifted his journal—a blue spiral notebook. "Uh. Real right now is too personal for me to tell the class."

Swoons and howls of taunting filled the air. Somebody tried to grab his journal. Some of the girls suggested what might be written on those coveted pages. But Cort just looked adorably shy, Rachel thought, except when those brown eyes met hers. Then he looked hot.

"Personal's what we want," Miss Tingey said. "And unless it's obscene, I expect you to share it. Maria's was personal, don't you think?"

The class agreed, and soon they were chanting, "Read, read, read."

Rachel joined in. She wanted more than anyone to know what Cort had written. He spoke with the reluctance of doing something he really didn't want to do but knew he wouldn't get out of.

"Real is proving to Rachel Baxter that all jocks aren't jerks."

The room thundered with screeches of approval and laughter. Some of the guys slapped Cort's palm.

Rachel buried her head in her crossed arms on her desk and tried to stop laughing. Her face burned. People patted her back, somebody tickled her and she jerked upright.

"Okay," Miss Tingey laughed. "I guess you two have something to work out."

"Rachel should read what's real," a boy suggested.

Shaking her head, Rachel said, "Never."

"That's not fair," Cort protested, his playful smirk aimed her way.

Rachel slapped her journal shut. That's all she'd need, to read aloud her feelings for Cort. Thankfully, Miss Tingey moved on to other students, but Cort still grinned at her.

Subtly he mouthed, "Later."

The movement of his lips sent a pleasant shudder right down her center. She gave him a non-committal shrug.

After class, Cort followed Rachel. "What's in your journal, Rache?" he asked. She caught a whiff of something rich and heavenly he'd sprayed on. His brown eyes sparkled.

"You'll never know."

"I shared mine."

"How nice for you. Can we change the subject now?"

"Why? You look pretty when you're embarrassed."

Heat flushed her cheeks. He was charming, another point for Cort Davies. "I bet you say that to all the girls."

"Nope." He opened the door to the locker hall for her and she passed, stealing a glimpse of his muscled arm. "You'd like to think I say that to all the girls though, right?"

Her friends were approaching and she felt a stab of dread that this choice moment would soon be gone. "Maybe."

"You'll tell me when I've proved you wrong?"

He was so cute, his face so sincere. Rachel had doubts she'd ever tell him because then all of this would be over.

"Rache." She was surrounded now, albeit apprehensively, by the guys, guardedly checking out Cort.

"Hey." Cort greeted them casually. Then he looked at her again. "So I'll see you tonight?"

"Sure."

Cort walked away but the fluttering in her stomach didn't leave. She watched as he melded into the crowd.

"You know Cort Davies?" Sam asked.

Todd's expression was wounded. "Are you going to the dance with him?"

Rachel walked the opposite direction. "I'm not going to the dance, I already told you."

"But he said he'd see you tonight." Todd fell instep with her, his frustration plain.

Rachel refused to let it bug her. "That's what he said."

"So, what does that mean?" Todd persisted.

"Leave it, dude." Sam elbowed him.

"What, Rache?"

Rachel stopped and glared at Todd. "Are you my big brother now or something? My personal life is private." She saw Ticia approaching and started toward her.

"Okay, okay," Todd snapped. "Sorry I asked."

"Don't ask again." Rachel turned to Ticia. "Where do you want to go?"

Sensing the air was thick with something, Ticia looked from face to face. The guy's heads lowered.

"Maybe we should go to lunch by ourselves." Rachel shot Todd a look.

The guys mumbled in protest and Todd shook his head.

"Fine."

"Fine," Rachel said, and led Ticia from the crowded hall.

Rachel stripped off her pink hoodie as she stormed through the parking lot. Ticia tried to keep up with her. The spring sun pulsed through thin wispy clouds, lighting the blue sky to near white. All around them students made a break for their cars.

"What was that all about?" Ticia waited for Rachel to pop the locks on the car doors.

"That was Todd getting in my face for the last time." Rachel got in, started the engine.

"What? He still getting over the dance thing?"

"He's still getting over his ego thing." Rachel revved the engine before pulling out. "He thinks he owns me—seriously. All the guys do."

"They're just protecting you."

"From what? That's just plain stupid."

"They're jealous."

"But we're all friends."

"I know. But you know Todd's had it for you for a while."

"He knows I don't feel the same. Do I have to come right out and say it?"

"Yeah, maybe."

She'd hate to have to do that. Rachel's cell phone vibrated and she stuck it to her ear. "Hey, Jenn….When I didn't see your car, I figured you weren't coming. Call me later. Okay. See ya." Rachel dropped the phone on the seat.

"Let me guess, Jenn's going to lunch with John."

Rachel shot her a smile. "Of course."

"Oh, look." Ticia pointed to Kippers Fish and Chowder House where Cort was just hopping out of his white truck, followed by Ben and Chad.

"Carmel and Brownie are looking fine today," Ticia said. "Should we?"

The girls exchanged playful grins. Rachel pulled her car next to Cort's white truck just as they boys entered the restaurant. "Is this too obvious?"

Ticia had one leg out the door. "I don't think so."

"Yes, it is. I just saw him five seconds ago in the hall." Rachel searched the place, couldn't see through the reflection in the glass. "It looks like I'm following him."

"What do you care what it looks like? It's never bothered you before. And we need to eat somewhere."

Rachel's fingers tapped on her steering wheel. But timing was important. If she moved too fast, showed too much interest too soon; let him know too much about her too fast, that could kill things. She started the car.

Ticia whined. "Carmel and Brownie are in there. You may have seen Cort, but I haven't seen Carmel yet. Come on, for me."

Rachel looked at the window, wishing she knew if they'd been spotted or not. If they had, Cort might wonder why they weren't coming in. Ticia's light blue eyes begged.

Reluctantly Rachel got out, her chest filled with wild birds. There were dozens of places kids from school ate at during lunch break; Wendy's being the number one pick. Purple Turtle was another hot spot. She hoped Cort wouldn't think this was a set up.

They walked in and the smell of crisp, fried food scented the air. Pictures of light houses and oceans lined the wood-planked walls. Heavy rope, wooden steering wheels and plastic seagulls in flight hung from the ceiling.

Cort was taking his tray to the table when she caught his eye. Suddenly all of his friends looked at them. Cort waved. "Come sit," he called over the noise.

It only took a heartbeat to say yes. Rachel and Ticia ordered then joined the guys at a corner table.

"I thought you might say no," Cort told her as he pulled out a chair for her and she sat.

"Why would I say no?"

He sat next to her. "You're the most evasive girl I've ever met, Rache." Because the table was small and crowded, their bodies sandwiched next to each other.

"Am not."

"Are too." Cort reached over her, his arm brushing her shoulder as he grabbed her drink. "Is it okay if I call you Rache?"

"Sure."

"What do you drink, anyway?" He opened the plastic lid but Rachel stopped him, laying her hand over his.

"Try it," she told him, lifting the straw to his lips. His mouth surrounded the tip, keeping his eyes locked with hers, he drank.

"Something diet." He pulled back and made a face she thought was cute.

"I like it."

"I hate diet."

She took the drink, shrugged. Then she picked up his plastic cup, and pressed the straw to her lips, noticing how he sat perfectly still, watching. "Chocolate shake."

He took the shake and immediately put his lips where hers had been and took a deep sip. His voice was low, "Yup." He popped a fry in his mouth. "So, you eat here a lot?"

"Sometimes."

"See?" He shook his head. "See how vague you are? Drives me nuts."

"I don't do it on purpose."

Commotion had them looking toward the glass doors. A small group of elderly people shuffled in.

"Oh my gosh," Rachel stood. "Hey!"

Charlie looked over. He was a nurse's assistant at Countryside. Mannie, Lily and another woman Rachel had seen occasionally at her readings was with him. Their wrinkled faces broke into giant smiles when they saw her.

"Your grandma?" Cort asked.

Rachel slid out of her chair. "No. I'll be right back." Quickly she made her way over and helped Charlie seat them.

"What's our lovey doing here?" Mannie cupped her cheeks.

"Just eating lunch with some friends. What are you guys doing here?"

"Why it's Friday," Lily piped, "Fish day."

"We get to have a field trip on fish day," Mannie confided.

Rachel laughed.

"Thanks for helping," Charlie told her. "Ladies, I'll be

right back with your orders."

Rachel sat down at their table. "Where's Martin?"

Mannie made a face. "You know him, too prickly to leave his comfort zone. I told him he needs to get out once in a while but he says it's too late for that."

"Are you here with that young man?" Lily pointed a crooked finger Cort's direction.

"Uh, well, I'm here with some guys, yes."

"He's mighty handsome, I must say." Mannie looked over obviously. Cort sent them a friendly wave. "Mighty handsome."

Lily strained to see. "And what's his name?"

"His name is Cort."

Mannie patted her hand. "What a fine couple you'd make. Oh, look. Here he comes."

"Hi." Extending his hand, Cort carefully shook each of the elderly women's hands. "I'm Cort."

"We've heard so much about you," Lily beamed.

Cort shot Rachel two raised brows. "You have?"

Mannie grabbed his hand, held it firmly. "You take care of our girl now, you hear?"

Rachel wanted to dissolve into the floor.

"I most definitely will," Cort said.

"You come visit us with our lovey," Lily said. "I'm hungry, where's Charlie?"

"I'd better go." Rachel stood, kissed their cheeks. "See you soon."

Mannie squeezed her hand before she left. "Bye now."

Rachel walked back to the table with Cort without saying

anything. Too bad if he was blown away by her senior friends, but if he was then that was something she had to accept. Her friends at Countryside, her time spent with them, was more important than some flying leap with a guy.

She listened to Ticia flirting with Chad, who responded likewise. Surely Cort was man enough to handle a few old people, Rachel thought, stirring her straw in her drink. When he sat quietly for a time, she wondered if she'd finally add a strike against him.

After lunch, the boys walked them to the car. Ticia was all smiles and giggles when Chad opened her door and leaned through the open window to talk to her.

Rachel paused before she got in. "Guess I'll see you later." She saw nothing telling in Cort's eyes.

"Yeah." Cort held her door open and the breeze carried his scent into her car. She took in a deep breath and he shut the door.

Ticia was euphoric on the drive back to school. "I think Carmel's going to ask me out."

Absently, Rachel put her thumb nail between her teeth. Even with the hard acrylic she still chewed. Messages, looks, secrets—why did guys have to be so confusing and frustrating? Why did they have to play this game? She wondered if Mannie and pretty Lily had played games when they were young. Maybe Martin had never found anybody because he hadn't been willing to.

When did playing end and real begin?

EIGHT

Miss Chachi's was packed. Girls waited outside. Cort sweat under the pressure. There was no way he could do all of the fills, pedicures and anything else the clients wanted by himself.

He asked Miss Chachi to help him deflect some of the girls to Misu, Tiaki, Abby and Jasmine but she was reluctant, telling him he was the reason the girls had come. He needed to work faster so their clientele would grow.

He hadn't gotten up for any pee breaks and his back teeth were beginning to float.

Some of the waiting girls ran out of time and had one of the other nail technicians do their jobs. Cort tried to ignore Miss Chachi's glares of displeasure when that happened, but she paced the center aisle like a drill sergeant, watching everyone work.

Loud laughter by the door caused Cort to look up from his current nail job. Bree flounced in, followed by Shaylee and Megan. They pushed their way through the crowd until they were at his table.

"Hi, Cortie."

She was dressed in a white tube dress that glittered from

head to toe. Her curvy body looked just the way he imagined she wanted it to look—everything shockingly outlined.

"Hey."

"I broke a nail," she whined. "Can you fix it real quick?"

He looked around at those waiting. "Does it look like I can fix it?"

Bree didn't even glance. "I'm all ready and they still have to get dressed. I should go first since I'm closer."

He jerked his head toward the front where the seats were all taken. "Get in line, Bree."

Beads of sweat sprouted at his hairline, down his spine. His pits were drenched.

Bree shot a saccharine smile at the girl whose nails he was doing. "Can I just cut in for a quick sec?"

Cort looked up, annoyed. "Bree, I'm in the middle of an appointment."

"I see that, but she can go to the bathroom or something. Who is she, anyway?"

The girl was speechless, staring from Cort to Bree. "It's okay," the girl finally said and stood.

"No." Cort reached for her.

"Really, it's okay." She eased by Bree with the respect Bree's popularity demanded.

Bree sat with a satisfied smile and extended her hand. "See? It's a little chip and it'll catch on my dress and, oops—what if it rips and my dress falls off?"

"You'd like that, wouldn't you?" Cort took her finger.

Bree's bare, glittering shoulders lifted. "Would you?"

The idea shot heat through him, whether he wanted it or

not. With a cotton ball soaked in acetone he wiped her nail clean. "I won't be there to see it."

"It could happen anywhere. Even here."

He filed the nail and kept his mouth shut, trying not to think of Bree without a dress.

"You know, you and I should be going to this dance together," she chattered. "It'd be fun, don't you think? We're like such buds and all."

He didn't answer.

"Sometimes I like being with friends, you know? Friends that know me and that I can hang with." She wiggled. "And then, of course, if something *happens* with that friend, well, that's cool, too.

"I mean, you and I know each other well enough that if something *did* happen, it would totally rock, you know? Cause, we'd be like, cool with it and all."

Cort only lifted his eyes to hers for a second, but in that second, female interest was alive and well. The desperation in her eyes caused him to look away. He wasn't interested, and even though Bree wasn't his type, he wouldn't hurt her feelings and say so.

"So you never asked the mystery girl?" Bree inquired.

"It was too late." He buffed next. "Besides, I have to work."

Bree looked around. "What kind of a slave driver keeps a hot guy from going to the dance?"

"As you can see, my services are an integral part of the girls going to the dance."

"Your *services*?" Bree teased but didn't say more when

he shot a glare at her. "Maybe the mystery girl is going with someone else."

"She's not," he said simply and began to paint the first coat.

Bree looked at Shaylee and Megan who had kept respectfully quiet until now. "Well, she must not be anybody because everybody who's anybody is going. Except you, of course."

He blew on the wet nail, sliding her a narrowed look.

"Time to dry." Cort flicked on the mini fan next to her, and shoved her hand in front of it.

"Hey," she bit out, "careful there. You wouldn't want to pay for this dress to be dry cleaned because you got some polish smeared on it."

Cort leaned back and stretched tight muscles. Surveying the room, he saw even more of the waiting girls had finally given up and were being taken care of by other nail techs.

Then Rachel walked in. She was with Ticia and Jennifer.

He sat forward with a jerk that caused both Bree and Shaylee to turn around and look. Bree's eyes slit.

"Well, Jennifer's got John. That Ticia chick is just too ugly. That leaves...I see."

Cort grabbed Bree's hand and looked at her nails. "One more coat and you're good to go."

"You know, I heard that Rachel's a hooker."

His polish brush froze. "You're wrong."

"No, seriously," Bree continued with sordid delight. "She works the streets here in P.V. And she totally sleeps with those guys that hang with her." The sweat covering Cort's back heated again. Finishing the last coat, he pushed Bree's hand in front of the fan. "Shut up."

"Oh, I see." Bree grinned. "Shay, I think I know who Cort's mystery woman is. It's that Rachel Baxter chick."

Shaylee leaned close. "The one that hooks?" Bree nodded.

"She does not hook," Cort hissed. "And she doesn't sleep around." He looked at Rachel, checking in at the front desk with Miss Chachi. Doubt trickled into his mind—she *had* been out last night, her mother said she was working. "She's too rich to do anything like that," he half mumbled.

"Those guy friends of hers keep her wallet fat."

"That's crap," Cort shot. Rachel wasn't a hooker. She was perfect, wasn't she?

"I heard her mom used to, and she wouldn't let her do anything else but hook," Shaylee added.

"I'm sure it's true," said Bree. "Just look at her. What else could she do?"

They all looked over as Rachel strode down the aisle with Jennifer and Ticia by her side. "I heard her friend hooks, too," Bree whispered, "that Ticia one. Even though I can't see any guy hooking up with her, not for money, anyway. They probably have, like, a two for one deal."

Cort rolled his eyes.

"Hey." Rachel only looked at Cort, and that settled his whirling insides a bit.

Bree stood slowly, her eyes scanning Rachel from head to toe. Cort couldn't wait until she and her tribe were gone. She blew on her nails then jerked her head at Shaylee, who jumped to attention, reached in Bree's purse, brought out

Bree's wallet and handed it to her. Bree glared at her friend
before plucking out five dollar bill and dropping it on Cort's
table. "I think five is more than enough for today. Bye,
Cortie. Don't say we didn't warn you." She cackled out a
laugh when she reached the door.

* * *

A few hours later, most of the crowd was gone. Misu sat
at the base of one of the pedicure chairs, wiping the vinyl
cloth clean. At another table, Jasmine finished up a full set,
while Abby swept. Miss Chachi stood dutifully up front,
counting cash.

Cort gestured to Rachel to sit in the chair facing him
while he pulled another chair alongside for Ticia. Miss Chachi
had talked Jennifer into a complimentary foot massage, and
she sat with bliss on her face, while Tiaki squished and pulled
her feet and toes.

"You're busy," Ticia said, awe lining her voice.

Cort couldn't have made it to the dance even if he'd been
set to go. He was beat. Rubbing his knuckles, Cort readied his
tools for Rachel's job and let out a sigh. "Yeah. It's been crazy
today."

The fatigue on his face worried Rachel. "I can come
back another day." She stood but he snapped out a hand and
stopped her.

He shook his head. "It's okay. Sit."

"You look wasted."

He reached out for her hands and his eyes sharpened, making something inside of her heat. She set her hands in his and he began to rub his fingers over hers in a soothing, circular motion.

"Just a fill then?," he asked.

She nodded. He examined her nails. "Pretty good job." Then he looked up, smiled. "But mine will be better." He wiped away the white tips with acetone. "How come you ladies aren't going to the dance?," he asked.

"I'm going," Jennifer piped from the pedicure chair. "We're just going late."

"You and John, right?" Cort asked.

Jennifer nodded, coloring to a shade of pink.

"That's cool. He's a cool guy. What about you ladies?"

"Didn't get asked," Ticia said.

"By the right guys," Rachel added.

"If Carmel had asked me, I'd have gone." Ticia dug into her purse and brought out a compact. "I still don't know if he's going."

"I didn't hear," Rachel said. "But I know for a fact Brownie isn't. And since—"

"Carmel. Brownie?" Cort dropped the saturated cotton ball into the trash. He took her hands again.

The girls broke out in laughter. "That's what we call these really hot guys we know."

Ticia blotted her nose. "That way we can talk about them anytime, anywhere and no one knows what we're saying."

Cort grabbed the electric sander. "Who's Brownie and

Carmel?"

"Like we'd tell you," Rachel said.

He turned on the sander and sanded her nails. "Why not? Or can I guess?"

"You can guess but we won't say."

"Top secret," Cort mused. "The hottest guys…well, I'm not the one to judge that, I guess."

"Oh, come on, let's see who you think is hot," Jennifer teased.

His cheeks reddened. "I don't think we look at guys the same."

"Obviously," Rachel tilted her head. "Give it a shot. Come on."

He finished sanding, set the tool back in its holder and thought for a moment. "Hmm. Most girls I know think John's a celebrity."

"And he's taken," Jennifer piped.

Cort nodded. "Chad and Ben are pretty cool." He watched their faces for any sign that he'd hit the target. "I mean, they're always stocked with women, you know?"

Ticia broke into a laugh. "Yeah, we know."

"Kevin and Eric are pretty popular too. Am I right?"

Rachel watched as he took her hands again, rubbing his thumbs over her sanded nails. "They're nice guys," she said.

He started the fill. "But you're still not going to tell me."

"No." Because his head was bowed, his eyes focused on her nails, Rachel took the opportunity to shoot the girls a wink.

"So," Rachel began, to Ticia. "You coming to work with

me tomorrow night?"

Cort's head jerked up. He looked at both girls, then over at Jennifer, lying back with her eyes closed. He thought about what Bree had suggested—the outrageous idea that they were hookers. His cheeks burned with the ridiculousness of it and he got back to work.

"I don't know if I can," Ticia said.

"It won't take that long. We can spend as much time as we want."

"I know."

"I thought you liked doing it," Rachel said. Cort's eyes widened.

"And I hear you're good at it, Ticia," Jennifer added.

Ticia nodded. "I do like it. It's just that, well, I was hoping to hook up with Carmel, you know?"

"How about afterwards?" Rachel asked.

"I'm usually tired after. I mean, for some reason it really drains me being around those guys."

Cort kept his head low. Could it be true? They couldn't be talking about—no way. His gut started to churn.

"But they need us." Rachel glanced from her nails to Ticia as she talked. "Think of the service we're providing."

Cort's mouth fell, but he stayed focused on Rachel's nails.

"But I thought you just did it the other night?" Ticia asked.

"I did." When Cort's grip turned hard, she looked at him. "Easy there."

"Sorry," he mumbled. He couldn't look at her, not when she was talking about hooking like it was nothing. His churning stomach twisted into a fist.

Rachel went on, "Martin likes the hard stuff."

"No romance for him, I know," Ticia said.

"Ouch!" Rachel pulled back her hand.

"I'm sorry," Cort reached for her. "I—I'm just tired."

"I should come another day."

He gently pulled her hand over. "No, it's okay. Really."
He started to work again, trying to dismiss the disgust he felt.

"Anyway," Rachel continued. "Oh, guys, I saw Sunshine today."

Ticia nodded enthusiastically. "He said hi to me in the hall."

"He's so sweet," Rachel said.

"He was with Penguin."

Cort looked up. "Penguin? What, the guy have some sort of funny walk?"

The girls laughed. It helped, but he was still in turmoil about what he overheard.

"Actually, he does," Rachel said. "But it's not, like, weird or anything—just cute."

How could girls who did something as crazy as make up funky code names for guys double as hookers in Pleasant View? It didn't make sense.

"Ouch." Rachel pulled her hand away again. "You pinched my finger."

"Sorry, sorry." Cort took her hand back. "I'll be gentler, I promise."

"Something wrong?" Rachel asked.

"No. Sorry. Really."

"Do you hurt all your clients?" she teased.

"Uh, no." He kept his head lowered. With the nails formed, he sanded, buffed and readied them for white-tip paint.

"Think about tomorrow night," Rachel finally said to Ticia. "We can meet or I can pick you up."

"If I don't get my wish and hook up with Carmel, then I will. What will you do?"

Rachel shrugged, watching Cort spray a white tip. She made sure he wasn't looking before she shot a secret look at Ticia, then at Jennifer that spoke of hope. "You have any plans tomorrow night?" she asked him.

He looked up, surprised. "Me? Uh." If she really was hooking, Cort didn't want anything else to do with her. "I might be busy."

Rachel's smile faded. "Oh."

"Sounds like you're going to be busy anyway," he said.

"Just for a little while."

A little while? He swallowed a hard knot. "I wouldn't want to interrupt whatever it is you have going on. Sounds pretty important," he said.

"It is, but it's not going to take the whole night."

Jeez. Wham bam thank you M'am. Cort was angry and disappointed. She was too beautiful, too intelligent to give herself away. And what kind of mother allowed that, encouraged it even? The idea was too bizarre.

"I don't know." His tone was sharper than he intended. Her smile withered. He took her hands, looked at her nails. "I'll just do another coat of clear and you'll be done."

He'd changed like hot water to cold. Rachel glanced at her friends wondering what had happened. Wondering if she'd said something. Ticia shrugged. Jennifer's face was blank. Any hopes of hinting to hang out tomorrow night after her visit to Countryside were gone.

Maybe it was all the talk about other guys. Maybe he—well, he wouldn't be jealous; there wasn't enough between them to warrant that. Maybe he thought her hands were gross. *Too fat or something. Guys notice stuff just like girls do.* Was her breath bad? She'd just chewed gum and she still tasted mint. Whatever it was, he was coolly quiet and she tried not to let it get to her.

After he painted the last coat, Rachel carefully set her nails in front of the fan. He sat back, brows knit tight, eyes dark with something.

"So." He crossed his arms over his chest. "How do you know the old people?"

"They're friends."

"Friends?"

The sarcasm in his voice made her defensive. "Yes, friends. You have a problem with that? What? You don't you like old people?"

"Of course I like old people." He sounded just as defensive. "Who doesn't?"

"Well I can't see Bree or Shaylee or Megan hanging with them."

He sat forward, eyes feisty. "No, I can't either." He

studied her so intensely; she didn't know what to say and suddenly wished her nails were dry so she could get out of there.

"They're friends of yours, though, right?" she asked with a bite.

"Oh, so that means I don't do well with old people either, is that what you're saying?"

Rachel shrugged. She didn't like him being mean. It hurt, in fact. But she could be mean back. "Birds of a feather."

His jaw tightened. "I'm not like Bree, or Shaylee or any of them."

"Then why do you hang with them?"

"Why do you do what you do?," he snapped.

Rachel sat back, confused. "What?"

He stood. "Forget it. You're done—I mean, you're dry."

She met his frustration when she stood. "Great. Thanks." Thrusting her purse at Ticia, she didn't take her eyes from his. "Get out my wallet, will you?"

The air thickened. Ticia dove for the wallet. Jennifer scrambled off the pedicure chair and slipped on her shoes.

Rachel opened her wallet and threw two twenties on the table. "Thanks."

Then she turned and started toward the door, her friends on either side of her.

"You're welcome!" Cort stared at the money, every muscle draining with disappointment. Had the money come from her...job? The idea sickened him. After a moment, he picked it up and stuffed the bills in his front pocket.

NINE

Cort still couldn't believe Rachel had sat there and all but made her appointments while he did her nails. It was despicable and fascinating at the same time.

After the girls left, Miss Chachi locked the front door and turned off the red, electric OPEN sign.

"Busy day," she said.

Cort had never been so wiped. Hours of listening to girls gossip, complain and bicker was more exhausting than any football game he'd ever played. His hands ached. He flexed his fingers, massaged his knuckles as Miss Chachi surveyed the salon, gradually heading his way.

Quickly he tidied his area setting his brushes, pots and bottles where she had told him to. She stopped at his table, looked at his work place then up at him. For a flash, he caught something dark and unidentifiable in her black eyes. It startled him, but he smiled, and felt better when she did too.

"Good day today, yes?"

He nodded.

"You bring us lots of business. That is good. Keep it up."

He thought if he worked any harder, his fingers would fall off. Reactively, he flexed them again, and Miss Chachi looked at them. "You soak in ginger like I say?"

He shook his head. "We don't have any of that stuff."

She held up a finger indicating he should wait then disappeared behind the beaded curtain hanging in the opening to the back. He looked around; the other girls had gone he guessed, because they weren't anywhere to be found.

Rubbing his face with his aching hands, he let out a sigh. He was sick about Rachel. So much for proving he wasn't a jock like every other jock—she wasn't like anybody else either, for that matter.

"You soak in this tonight." Miss Chachi placed a baggie with mixed brown powders in his hand. "You feel better in the morning. I promise."

He nodded, tucking the bag into his pocket. He felt the money Rachel had given him, and took out the twenty he owed Miss Chachi. "This is for that last job," he told her. He wished Rachel had never come in. He wished he didn't know her dirty little secret.

Miss Chachi nodded, taking the bill. "I have something for you." She scuttled up front, grabbed a small paper and returned to him. "Your work permit." She handed it to him.

"Oh." He looked at it.

"You hang, right there on wall." She pointed and gave him a thumb tack.

He tacked the paper to the wall, feeling a little surge of pride. "Cool."

She nodded, looking from the permit to him. "Yes. Cool."

"Well, I guess I'll be off." He grabbed his keys out of his

drawer. "See you tomorrow."

"We need talk. Come."

He followed her to the front desk with dread. Surely she wasn't going to make him work more hours. She looked at the large, flat paper that had the schedule on it. "You come in all day tomorrow?"

"But I just worked tonight."

"Yes." She nodded. "But the clients all ask for you and look," she pointed to the paper. Every hour filled from nine until nine. "Full day.

He shifted and let out a sigh. "But the other girls can take—"

"—They can," she interrupted him and her tone was sharp. "They will. But some of these come tomorrow because they couldn't get you today. You see? We must please them."

The thought of another day like he'd had today tired him. "How long will this be like this? I have a life, you know."

Her black eyes narrowed. "Not much longer, Cort. Trust me."

Somehow, he couldn't bring himself to believe in her words. Maybe it was just that he was so wiped. He wanted to crash.

He drove home, checking the empty, darkened streets for Rachel. Was she working them tonight? The idea was so preposterous, he almost laughed out loud. One look around and he knew the rumor couldn't be true—there wasn't a soul in sight but the occasional car.

Once he turned onto Canyon Road there were a few more cars than usual. But then it was Friday night, and that meant kids everywhere. No lone men roamed the streets as his imagination had conjured.

When he got home, he realized he was starving. Somehow, he hadn't gotten a break at work what with dozens of clients waiting. He headed right to the refrigerator, opened it. And wanted to cry. Nothing but fruit and vegetables and something made of tofu and greens he didn't recognize filled the shelves.

"Where have you been?"

He turned; his mother stood in her robe. She peered at him over glasses perched half-way down her nose. In her arms was her usual stack of briefings. She set them on the counter, her face concerned as she came to him.

"You look tired." She pressed her hands to his face to feel for a temperature.

"I'm fine, Mom."

"Well, you don't have a fever." She picked up her papers. "There's dinner in there. Tofu Mexican casserole."

His stomach rolled. "Sounds great."

Cocking her head at him she considered. "You might be anemic."

"I'm just tired."

"Working hard on the job—that's good. Keeps the blood flowing. That keeps digestion turned up."

Wearily, he nodded and looked back into the refrigerator wishing he had the energy to go back into town and grab a burger.

"Get some rest. Your body is still growing. Sleep, good nutrition, and plenty of exercise."

Again he nodded.

She left and he shut the fridge door, the grumbling in his stomach loud. Then he heard the unmistakable crunch of chips being chewed.

He whirled. Lizzie stood in the doorway with a grin and a bag of Doritos. He almost lunged for them.

She darted out of his reach, laughing. "Get your own bag."

"Where did you find that?" he whispered.

"Had one of my friends pick it up for me." She held out the bag and he reached for it again but she snatched it back. "Tell me about Rachel."

That came out of nowhere. "Why do you want to know?"

"She called a minute ago."

He made another grab for the bag but she twisted away. "She your new girlfriend?"

Just thinking about Rachel, about that whole sordid story, made him angry and he made another grab for the chips, this time wrapping his sister in a tight squeeze trying to wrestle it from her. "Give me the chips."

"For – get – it," she grunted, struggling.

"I'm starving."

"I – don't – care!" Her smaller body wiggled free and she danced out of reach with a teasing smile that made him growl.

"Rachel as in Rachel Baxter?"

"No."

Lizzy dangled the bag in front of his nose and his shoulders drooped on a heavy sigh. "Forget it." He resigned himself to a night of starvation but she followed him back to the fridge.

"Okay, okay." She held out the bag. Greedily he took it.

"Easy there, pup."

"If you'd been chained to a chair, forced to listen to girl's gossip and whine for five hours without a break to take a leak, or eat, or anything else, you'd be a bear too." The first chip was pure heaven. He closed his eyes and moaned. "Man these are good."

Lizzie laughed. "They're just chips. Who's this slave driver you're working for?"

"Miss Chachi." He sat at a barstool and took another chip out, staring at it as if it were gold, before placing it in his mouth.

"And you're taking it?" Reaching over, Lizzie stole a chip. "That doesn't sound like you."

"I was broke, Liz. A year without a job will do that. I've gotta save up."

"Still," she crunched. "This is America."

"But she's not from here."

"So?"

He shrugged. "Her work ethic is more sweatshop, I guess."

"Boy, have you changed."

He didn't like her implication. "What do you mean?"

"The Cort Davies I knew wouldn't just roll."

"Well sometimes you just have to suck it up, and obviously you haven't figured that out yet." She reached for another chip but he jerked the bag out of her reach. "It's a sign of maturity," he told her.

"Yeah, right." She stood, wiped her hands on her jeans. "Whatever. That chick called."

He paused before taking another bite. "What did she say?"

"Just, 'tell him that Rachel called.' It's Rachel Baxter, isn't it?"

He wondered if his sister had heard any of the strange rumors. "You had a class with her, right?"

She nodded, taking a soda from where it was hidden in the further most cabinet.

"You sneak," he condemned.

"A girl's gotta eat." She popped off the top. "I know her, yeah."

"What's she like?"

Lizzie took a drink. "Totally cool. Really nice. Not like the gossiping snots I've seen you hang around."

"I do not." He grabbed for her Coke.

"Oh, since when are Bree and her pack of friends anything but a bunch of self-serving wenches?"

"One drink, come on, Liz." He grabbed again before she handed it to him.

"So." He drank, wiped his mouth. "You haven't heard anything weird about Rachel?"

"What kind of weird?"

He handed her back the drink with a shrug. "Anything."

"She's rich, that's all I know. And, like, is an actress. She's, like, really good."

He bet that. He'd been fooled. He guessed everybody else was fooled too.

Lizzie suddenly stilled, looking over his shoulder. "Shh—I think Mom's coming."

Cort darted for the nearest cabinet and tossed the chips into it while Lizzie held the soda behind her back as their mother entered.

She looked at them both over the rim of her glasses. "What are you two doing?"

"Going to bed." Cort started toward the stairs but she sniffed.

"I smell something," she said, moving as she sniffed until she was right in front of the two of them. "Something smells like Doritos." She looked from one to the other. "Where's the bag?"

Lizzie shook her head. Their mother raised her eyebrow. "Is that what you think of my dinner?"

When neither Lizzie or Cort said anything, she looked at them deciphering. "I'll allow one cheat and this is it. As of this moment however, cheating's over. What kind of mother would I be if I ignored the facts—healthy nutrition leads to healthy lives. Now get to work on that essential eight hours you need for your still-growing bodies," she told them. She grabbed an empty mug from the glass cabinet and went on her way.

Lizzie looked after her, bringing her soda back around. "You think her sense of smell has like gotten sharper with this tofu thing?"

"No doubt." Cort stuffed the bag of chips under his shirt. "Lock up."

"That's not my job," Lizzie complained.

He shot her a grin over his shoulder as he headed to his room. "It is tonight. And you thought I rolled."

TEN

The message window was open on his Facebook page. Cort sat down and clicked it open. Rachel. The endless stream of Doritos he'd just consumed turned to rocks in his stomach.

RACHEL: you there?

He debated getting into anything more with her. He was still weighing what Bree and Shaylee had told him against what Lizzie said, and then there was what Lizzie had said about Bree and Shaylee to consider.

Recently he wondered about Bree and her friends. Being a guy, he only saw one side to her; a flirty, friendly vixen. But after listening to her rag in the salon, he started wondering how nice she really was.

Rachel, on the other hand, appeared to be everything he fantasized she would be—until today. The nasty rumor ate at him. He wanted the truth but he didn't have the nerve, or couldn't be mean enough, to confront her directly.

He had to find another way.

CORT: hey.

RACHEL: hey, did you suck in too many fumes or something?

CORT: no.

RACHEL: OK. but u r mad at me 4 some reason.

CORT: it was u that threw my $ down on the table.

RACHEL: i wasn't mad at u

CORT: so what was it?

RACHEL: u tell me.

Rachel stared at the screen, waiting. Ever since she'd left Miss Chachi's she'd been bugged. She ran their conversation over and over in her head and saw no reason for Cort to turn lame on her. She'd gone from mad to sorry to afraid and back to mad again. With some time to consider the future, which looked totally destroyed, she rotated back to fear.

She didn't like that. Fear meant she cared too much, and that her heart was the next thing to take a hit. But she couldn't get Cort's face out of her mind and that was enough for her to try to suck it up and figure out what had happened.

RACHEL: did i say something?

It's not what you said, it's what you *do*, Cort thought but couldn't type it. Instead, he wrote:

CORT: forget it. how are the nails?

RACHEL: awesome. u did a great job. if they don't lift, u'll have a new customer

CORT: more proof ?

RACHEL: you're still proving? good. 4 a minute i thought i might have scared u off

CORT: u don't scare me

In fact, now that he'd decided his plan of action, he wasn't concerned about anything. He'd find out for himself if she was walking the streets under the lamplight. Tomorrow night.

RACHEL: some guys have told me i do.

CORT: some guys don't have any balls.

RACHEL: Okaaaaaayyyy i won't go there.

CORT: tell me who carmel and brownie and sunshine are.

NYCBabe16: never.

CORT: do i have a code name?

Rachel grinned.

RACHEL: i'll think of one.

CORT: but you won't tell me, will you?

RACHEL: not on your life. let's see…puppy eyes…fast fingers…

CORT: *FAST FINGERS?*

RACHEL: better forget that one.

CORT: stud works

RACHEL: u wish.

CORT: guess i have to prove that, too.

Rachel enjoyed a delicious shiver. There were lots of names she could call a guy as perfectly packaged as Cort. Sizzlin'. Magic Hands. Magic Hands—she liked it. Heat flushed in her hands as if he'd just touched them, like when he so gently massaged her fingers.

RACHEL: i just thought of your name.

CORT: uh-oh. what?

RACHEL: i told u u'll never know.

CORT: what's fair is fair. i'm naming you then.

RACHEL: go ahead.

What kind of name would he choose? How did he see her?

RACHEL: OK. i may give in. if u tell me, i'll tell u

CORT: i knew u'd want 2 know.

RACHEL: i just want to see what u'd come up with, that's all.

CORT: deal?

RACHEL: i'd better go. dad's on the phone and i want to talk to him.

CORT: OK.

RACHEL: what are you going to do now?

CORT: lie in bed and think about what to name you.

After they said goodbye, Rachel pictured him. Though she'd never set foot in his house, didn't even know where he lived, her imagination easily conjured up the scene of him in long, plaid flannel pajama pants and no shirt. That ripped bod gorgeously splayed with one arm over his head, muscles flexed while he was hard at work, thinking.

Rachel turned off her computer glad things between them were on a better wave. In spite of her resolve, she wanted something with Cort, even if it was only for him to continue on this crazy quest to prove to her he was solid—not jelly, like most jocks.

It would be cool if something more happened between them. It would rock everything if one day he kissed her. Her first kiss—more than a casual greeting. That's what she'd think about tonight.

Right after she talked to her dad.

ELEVEN

Because he was starving and hadn't been duped into
eating the tofu benedict his mother had prepared for him and
Lizzie that morning, the haunting scent of coffee pulled Cort
into Minerva's.

Poor Lizzie, he thought with a moment's amusement. At
least he had the excuse of a job to get him out of the house.

The bell over the door jingled when he entered. Half a
dozen girls he recognized from school sat at green wrought
iron cafe tables sipping steamers.

Minerva smiled from behind the counter. "Hey, Cort.
What can I get you?"

He greeted the girls, feeling like a bug under a
microscope as he crossed to the counter. "A Min's Special."

"With whipped cream?"

"That'd be great." He glanced around, nodding casually at
the girls still watching him. "You're busy," he said to Minerva.

"Thanks to you." She filled a Styrofoam cup with the
rich, dark chocolate—her special recipe. "To go, right?"

He nodded.

"They're all waiting for Miss Chachi's to open." She
sprayed on a generous mound of cream, sprinkled it with

109

cinnamon.

"They are?" He paid her and took the cup.

"Ever since you started work it's been great."

"Wow." He sipped, and scorched his upper lip.

"That's hot," she warned him. "I guess Miss Chachi loves you, huh? You want to come to work for me too?" she joked.

His hands warmed holding the hot chocolate. "She barely gives me time to breathe or I would."

"Well, it's been so slow down here. It's great to finally have some foot traffic. You keep it up." She went about clearing cups from the tables and Cort left the cafe, followed by some of the girls.

A guy could let this get to his head, he thought, knowing full well a line of girls trailing him was pretty cool.

He walked into Miss Chachi's and got ready to work.

"You very popular," Tiaki said with a smile as she set up at her table. "Miss Chachi like that."

"Yeah." He set down his cup and took off his coat. Miss Chachi was at the front desk, getting the first clients of the day settled. "How long have you known Miss Chachi?"

Tiaki glanced to the woman before answering. "She give me job. She know my family need me to work and send money back so they can come here to United States someday."

The news surprised him. "The other girls? Jasmine, Abby and Misu?"

"They same. She pay for us to come here, teach us nail and we send money to family."

Suddenly all of the money he'd made and spent on stupid stuff like the hot cocoa he was enjoying seemed like a waste. As he worked, all he could do was think about the girls and how little they made, how much he had made in comparison, and how much more they needed it.

Customers came for only him. He had to change that, for the sake of the girls. He started talking them up with his clients in the hopes those who couldn't fit in his schedule would choose one of the others and stick with her, so their individual client base would grow.

Half-way through the day, he took a break and went back to Minerva's, and grabbed each of the girls a gourmet fruit juice. He'd never seen any of them take a break. He'd only gotten the reprieve because he threatened mutiny.

As he walked back to the salon, he noticed Bree pull up in her pearly-white convertible. She had her usual offenders with her. Shaylee and Megan never did anything without dragging along on the hem of one of Bree's short skirts.

He couldn't believe he'd once thought Bree was hot. She was so different, now that he'd heard her talk, seen the way she was with other girls.

She got out of her car with her dark glasses on and waved at him. For the life of him, he couldn't figure out why she was there again. She'd come in every week since he'd started working.

"Cortie." She wore a velour sweat outfit in fawn. Her disheveled blonde striped hair was up in a claw. "Is one of those for me?" she asked, noticing the fruit juice in his arms. She reached for one, but he pulled back.

"Actually, no."

Pouting, she followed him into the salon. He ignored her

and passed out the juices to the girls. When Tiaki bowed her head in gratitude, he felt a slug of emotion in his chest.

"What are you doing here?" He sat down at his table.

"I want you to give me a pedicure and leg massage. After the dance, I need it. It was crazy."

"Jasmine does the pedicures."

"But I want you to do it. I'll pay double."

"I don't do pedicures, Bree." He was purposefully harsh so she got the message. She didn't say anything more, she marched directly to Miss Chachi.

"She's mad," Shaylee muttered.

"I don't give a crap," he said. But the crimp in his gut told him to be ready. Sure enough, Bree sauntered back with a smile on her face, followed by Miss Chachi whose face wore a frown.

"This young lady want pedicure from you, Cort. She willing to pay double. You do pedicure." She pointed to the large, stuffed chairs.

"But—"

"No but," Miss Chachi scolded. "Pedicure same as manicure. Soak, massage, clean, file and paint." She clapped her hands.

Begrudgingly, Cort moved to the big chair and waited for Bree to sit. Shaylee and Megan pulled up two empty stools next to her; *a queen with her servants*, Cort mused angrily.

Miss Chachi started the swirling hot water and patted Cort's shoulder. "Soak, massage, clean, file and paint. Easy." Then she left.

Bree stared at him, her shiny lips curled, her eyelids

heavy. "Take off my shoes, Cortie."

Every muscle in his face drew tight. He'd just love to shove her feet with her fancy flip-flops into the hot water. But he took her feet in his hands and slipped off the light-weight leather sandals without incident.

"Now roll up my pants," her voice dropped an octave. "Then they won't get wet."

Cort glanced at Jasmine who was in the middle of a pedicure and noticed that her client also had the legs of her pants rolled up to her calves. He leaned over and started rolling.

"You have great hair," Bree told him.

Heat singed his cheeks. He didn't say anything.

"Higher," Bree said and leaned close so their faces were within inches. "I want my massage all the way up."

Cort swallowed a lump in his throat. Part of him responded with an uncomfortable twist inside as his fingers brushed the tanned smoothness of her legs. He didn't like that.

He sat back. "Roll them yourself."

Bree's eyes narrowed. She finished the job, rolling and pulling the velour up to the top of her thighs. Then she extended her two tanned, long legs toward him. He couldn't help but look at them. They were great legs, no matter what he thought of who they belonged to.

Slowly she dipped her pointed feet primly into the water. "Ahh." She leaned back with a sigh, settling into the chair like a cat.

While her feet soaked, he watched Jasmine work. In slow,

circular motion, she rubbed cream into the girl's calves. His stomach fluttered. He'd never touched a girl that way before and wasn't sure he could do it without it affecting him in an embarrassing manner.

"Cortie," Bree taunted. He looked at her. "Put the cream in your hands," she instructed. "Since this is your first time," she ran her tongue around her lips nice and slow. "I'll be your tutor, how's that?"

He almost rolled his eyes. Instead, he squirted a little of the pink, flower-smelling stuff in his palms feeling like an idiot.

"Now." She lowered her voice. "Touch me."

Megan and Shaylee's eyes locked on him like he'd been stripped naked. He swallowed. Waited. Reluctantly, Cort put his hands on one of Bree's legs. His face felt like it was on fire and that fire spread everywhere else. Her leg was smooth as silk, without any bumps whatsoever. He was afraid. Afraid he'd rub too hard or not hard enough. Did he rub in circles? Lines? Use his fingers? His palms?

He glanced at Jasmine, now using her whole hand in the process, so he did the same.

"Mmm," Bree purred. "You're good at this."

Again, heat flushed through him. He couldn't look her in the eye, not when his hands were going places they had never gone before. Somehow it didn't feel right. A guy shouldn't be touching a girl like this unless they were an item.

"Who'd have known," Bree lulled, her eyes closed in bliss. "Cort Davies and his hands."

In a quick jerk he pulled back. "I can't do this."

"Yes you can," Bree shot out. "You were doing the best ever. Don't stop. It can't be that bad." Lifting her leg, Bree turned it temptingly before him. "I've been told I have great legs. Consider yourself lucky."

Cort licked his dry lips, saw Miss Chachi make her way over with a frown on her face and he put his hands back on Bree's calf and started rubbing.

"So." Bree settled back and looked at Shaylee. "Did you and Mark stay at a hotel last night?"

Shaylee shook her head. "He's saving for prom. But he did stay late. I snuck him out the basement door at four this morning. What about you and Ty?"

"He was so boring. I can't believe I went with him. Never again—I'm done with that loser. He looked good though, don't you think?"

Shaylee and Megan nodded.

"So at least the pictures will be perf." Bree's gaze stayed on Cort. "You and I should have gone, Cort. We'd have had so much fun."

He wanted to roll his eyes but didn't. He'd never go anywhere with her. He knew that like he knew he'd never do another pedicure for her.

"Higher," she told him when he stopped the massage at her knee.

He looked at her.

"Oh come on," Bree taunted. "Don't tell me you can't handle it." She laughed and so her friends did. He started on her other calf with his face averted.

"Wait!" Bree almost shouted. "Wait just a second! I don't

115

believe it. Don't tell me you've never—" She started laughing loud then, and the whole salon looked over. Cort kept his head low to hide his heated cheeks.

Bree tapped her feet in the water gleefully, and leaned toward him so her lips brushed his ear. "You're a virgin, aren't you? Cort Davies is a virgin."

Cort's heart pounded. Sweat sprung from every pore.

Bree sat back, eyes glittering with mischief. "Unbelievable."

"What?" Anxious, Shaylee leaned over. "What? Tell us."

Bree shook her head slowly, her eyes pinning Cort over lips spreading into a grin. "It's a little secret between Cort and me, isn't it, Cortie?"

His throat was tight so he swallowed. "I didn't know it was a secret." As if it wasn't any big deal, he started her massage again, but his fingers shook.

"Oh, yeah, right," Bree barked. Then she leaned close so only he could hear. "You're a virgin and a liar?"

He shot her a glare. "At least I don't spread myself around."

"I don't hear any complaints."

"Here's your first one."

"Don't complain until you've tasted for yourself," she whispered. She sat back with a sigh. A pain in his gut warned him this could get bad.

"You know what I think?" Bree stretched like a wicked kitten. "I think I'm going to take you out, Cortie—on me. It will be a date you'll never forget. That, I can promise you."

TWELVE

Darkness cloaked Pleasant View like the secret threatening Cort's social existence—the blackness came fast and cold, like a menacing fog, and when he finally said goodnight to Miss Chachi and the girls, all he could think about was Bree and her big mouth.

It was hard to concentrate on his plan for Rachel when Bree was out somewhere no doubt spilling the juice on him.

His closest friends already knew. Virginity was a secret they all shared. It was what it was, and Cort wasn't ashamed of it. Or hadn't been, until snaky Bree guessed. He was so tongue-tied from the newness of giving a pedicure he'd been unable to respond.

Still, he wouldn't lie to her. He'd get around it some how, though. The world didn't need to know his sexual status.

He got in his car.

A few weeks ago, he considered Bree a friend, someone he could easily go for if the moment was right. Every guy at school drooled over the cement she walked on. Pathetic. Couldn't any of them see beyond the fake California hair and tan?

He sat a moment in his car, unsure what to do next. He

felt trapped, and hated it.

His mother always said, what goes around comes around and if you live long enough, you get it all. He hoped it was true and that someone would give Bree what she deserved. For him, he'd focus on what he really cared about—finding out what Rachel did when she "worked."

He drove the quiet streets of Pleasant View looking for her. Where did she go? Did she stand on some corner, under a street lamp? Maybe she hung out at the pool hall or the local bar.

He slowed in front of Sadie's, looked in the windows, but it was just crowded enough, smoky enough, that he couldn't see inside. He parked and went in, knowing full well he'd get kicked out because of his age.

Smoke nearly choked him. He resisted the urge to wave a hand in front of his face. Something by Aerosmith blasted from a jukebox. Four guys and a girl, all with cigarettes hanging from their lips, surrounded a pool table. One leaned on his cue as another hung across the table taking a shot.

The bar was lined with men, some talking, some staring off into nothing as they nursed bottles or amber-filled glasses. The bartender took one look at him and started over. Cort quickly scanned the place for Rachel.

"You can't be in here." The pouch-bellied man without hair told him. His right ear winked with a gold hoop earring.

A woman appeared out of nowhere. She wore a tight red blouse and even tighter jeans. She eyed him, smiled. "Maybe he's older than he looks. Maybe he just has a baby face."

Cort stuffed his hands in his front pockets and drew

his lower lip between his teeth feeling like he was in a naked dream.

"How old are you, baby?" she asked.

"I'm looking for somebody," his voice cracked.

"I'm somebody." Her mascara-caked lashes resembled black fangs.

"Somebody else," he said.

She laughed. "I seen you around."

He inched backward toward the door. "I work over there," he pointed over his shoulder.

"Yeah? Where at?"

"Miss Chachi's."

"The nail place?"

He nodded, relieved to feel the door at his spine. The bartender was back behind the bar and he shouted, "Get the kid out of here, Brenda, 'fore I get arrested."

Brenda opened the door and stepped outside with him. "I met the lady. She's a funny little thing, isn't she?"

Cort nodded, taking fresh air into his lungs with a deep breath.

She eyed him with sincere concern. "Who you lookin' for, baby?"

"A girl." He looked around. There was no one in sight. Pounding music seeped from the walls of the pool hall and out into air around them.

"I haven't seen any your age down here tonight. You go to that place I seen the kids go, that Wendy's on State Street. That's where you'll find a girl for you."

He gave her a nod and gladly made his way back to his

119

car. He drove some more but Rachel was nowhere in sight.

The world of that pool hall was not his world and as he drove along, searching the streets, he wondered about that woman. Pleasant View was like any other small town, with its cozy neighborhoods lined with hundred-year-old trees and houses both archaic and brand new.

There wasn't a lot of crime here. He knew this first hand because his mother was a defense attorney for the city besides having her own practice. He wondered how those people in the bar liked living in a place as sheltered as Pleasant View. How a girl like Rachel Baxter, with her supposed night job, liked living here.

Then he saw her.

She was walking along 100 West—alone. Was she nuts? It was dangerous near the train tracks this time of night; anybody with a brain knew that.

He parked and got out, jogging until he was close enough to keep her in his sight, dart out of hers, and stay on her tail without losing her.

She wasn't wearing what he thought a hooker would wear, though he'd never seen one before. He'd seen plenty of movies with actresses wearing bright colors and flashy stuff. Here she was in conservative jeans and a dark turtleneck.

She held something under her arm and her walk was brisk. A car drove by and slowed but she didn't even look at it. Even when they rolled down the windows and he heard the unmistakable howling of male voices, she kept walking.

Soon, the car drove off and the two of them were again alone on the deserted road. The houses were the size of tiny boxes with the exception of Countryside Manor. Court thought the rest home looked like it belonged on some ranch somewhere in Texas.

Rachel headed straight for it.

Every now and then, leaves under his feet crunched and she turned. He ducked into the nearest bush or darkened spot until she continued on.

She must know some people down here, he thought once again in step behind her. And, once again the idea of her hooking sickened him. Until she walked up the sidewalk and directly into Countryside Manor.

He hid behind one of the giant oaks flanking the walk until she was inside. Then he stood out in the open and stared at the massive building. Why was she going to a retirement home at nine o'clock?

Too curious to leave it at that, he climbed the steps and opened the heavy double doors. It smelled like his grandpa's house and something used for cleaning.

A woman with grey hair piled on top of her head looked up at him from behind the front desk and smiled. "May I help you?"

"Does Rachel Baxter work here?"

The woman nodded in the direction of an open double door off the lobby. "She's in the gathering room."

"Can I?" he asked. She nodded.

Nerves twitching Cort approached the doors. He heard Rachel's voice, the cool tone both deep and heavenly and he peered in. She greeted a small semi-circle of senior citizens, shaking their hands, kissing their cheeks. He recognized them from Kippers Fish and Chips. He stayed safely hidden in the doorway.

"What's our lovey going to read to us tonight?" Mannie asked.

"I didn't bring the Dirty Dozen, Martin." Rachel sat down in the center chair and opened the loose-leaf binder in her lap.

The old gentleman huffed but didn't move. "Well I hope it's not a romance. Could you find us a suspense?"

"For you, I will."

The group quieted and Rachel's voice filled the air like the scent of hot chocolate. Cort stood motionless. This was what she did at night? Read to senior citizens? He would have broken into a laugh if guilt hadn't slugged him. How could he have thought for one second what Bree said was real?

He listened to Rachel change with the characters she brought to life and was overcome, utterly floored by this secret of hers.

But it really wasn't secret; she said she was friends with these good people. He saw the anxious way she left him and his friends to stop at their table for a visit that wasn't rushed. The friendly way she kissed their cheeks in goodbye. She was something else, Rachel was. That was real.

Most nights Rachel walked to Countryside Manor, like she did tonight, because the long walk gave her time to think. Tonight, she was bothered by the feeling that she wasn't alone. She'd walked this way a hundred nights and never felt threatened but a creepy skittering lodged in her spine. She looked around at every noise only to find a leaf dancing in the gutter, a cat crossing the street.

She neared Main Street and was glad. For what it was worth, what little went on there after sunset was better than the dead stillness of the neighborhood by the train tracks of Countryside Manor.

Passing the pool hall, the bang of loud country music clouded the air. She heard laughter, smelled smoke sneaking out the door. She passed without looking in and hurried on up the street, figuring if she ran into any trouble at all, it would be in the vicinity of the pool hall.

She still had a good mile to go until she was home, and that mile took her along quiet streets that weren't lit but for the occasional street light.

Her heart pounded when she heard another crackle. She turned, saw a shadow move into darkness and quickened her pace. Digging out her cell phone, she decided to call her mom for a ride.

The crunch of leaves, the soft pad of foot on pavement had her whirling around again.

"Rache?"

She gasped. "Cort?"

He moved into what little light streamed between thready clouds. "What are you doing? Following me?"

He shrugged. "Yeah, as a matter of fact. What are you doing?"

"Walking." She started up the street not sure if she should be annoyed or pleased he was following her.

"It's dangerous."

"We're in Pleasant View."

123

"And crime sometimes happens," he said. "My mom's a defense attorney for the city. She sees it."

"Oh, you mean the drunk who pees outside a building?"

"I'm serious."

Even in the faded moonlight the concern on his face was obvious. "Thanks for worrying."

They walked up the long stretch of road without talking for a while. As they ascended, homes grew larger, property more spacious. Fences popped up. An occasional car drove by. Rachel couldn't deny she felt better having Cort along.

"So," she began, "up to your elbows in hands today?"

He laughed. "It was brutal."

"Caressing girls' hands, talking to them, yeah, sounds real nasty."

"Seriously, I had no idea girls could be so…vicious."

"Oh, yeah. They're the mothers of cattiness. But then, you have a sister. I thought you knew that."

"I don't pay enough attention I guess. You have any brothers and sisters?"

She shook her head. "It's just me."

"Lucky you."

"Oh, come on, Lizzie's cool. I like her." He shrugged. "So what were you doing down here, you never said."

"Following you."

"Shut up."

"No, seriously."

"Why?"

"I wanted to…see you. Talk."

"You could have called me."

"I don't have your phone number yet."

"Oh, that's right."

"You can give it to me."

"Maybe. You could have messaged, saved yourself some time and energy, since the lions caught you in the den today."

He liked that she made him laugh easily. "You know, you think you really know someone and then – wham – you see them in another place and it's like, this huge shock."

"Bree?"

"How did you know?"

"Because girls that are two-faced are two-faced to girls as well as guys."

"I used to hang with her, you know? But lately I've just— she's changed."

Rachel laughed. "She hasn't changed, Cort. She's always been that way. You're just finally seeing her." A point for you, she thought. "I stay away from people like that."

"Smart. So, do you have a boyfriend?" he asked.

"I wouldn't flirt with you if I did," she said.

"But all those guys you hang with."

"All just friends. You have girls you're friends with and nothing else, don't you?"

"Yeah, but—"

"It works both ways, Cort."

"But I know guys, and guys don't spend time with a girl unless they're hoping for something more—"

"Don't disgust me." She shoved at him.

"It's true."

"Well my friends don't want anything from me."

"Oh, uh-huh. Okay. You just go on believing in fairy tales."

"You don't think girls are the same?"

"Logic tells me they might think the same but I have no clue about the female mind."

"You?"

"Jock, right?"

"Superficial jock," she corrected.

"So, is that what you think? You don't hang with girls unless you want something?"

He shrugged. "I'm no different than any other guy. But I have girls that I'm only friends with."

"So do I, have guys that I'm only friends with."

"And they surround you – constantly."

It pleased her that he was annoyed by this. "They protect me."

"Want you all for themselves is more likely."

Playfully, she slugged him again. They turned down a street lined with large, picturesque houses sitting on sprawling lawns.

"Is this your street?" he asked.

She pointed to a house lit up with dreamy yard lanterns. The place looked to be stone and brick, with bay windows and black shutters. "Nice house." Cort let out a whistle.

He walked her up the curved drive around the back. He could see a deck, pool, and a yard disappearing into trees. "Pool parties, cool."

"You'll have to come hot tubbing," she said, typing her code into the security pad that unlocked the back door.

"Want to come in?"

He'd gone from thinking she was a hooker to being invited inside her house in the matter of one hour. He wanted to laugh—at himself. But it was late, and he still had a long walk back to his car. He shook his head.

"Just answer me this one question," he started, leaning a shoulder in the door jamb. There was barely any light, but her skin was luminescent, like a sheath of pearls. Her large blue eyes looked black with wonder. And those lips—he so wanted to kiss them.

"Okay," she said.

"Am I there yet?"

She tilted her head. "Close, but not yet."

He smiled. Good, he thought, because I don't want this to be over, not by a long shot. She reached out her hand and his blood skipped through his veins.

"Come on." The next thing he knew, her soft, warm hand was around his and he was helpless not to follow her.

* * *

They sat outside. Stars sprinkled the onyx heavens as if an artistic hand had flung them like dust. A faint breeze rustled the trees surrounding the deck. Rachel sat in a flowered lounge chair while Cort swung idly from the hammock, strung between two deck posts.

"So," Rachel started.

Magic Hands • Jennifer Laurens

"So."

He looked hot lying there in the hammock. The way the moon lit his face, the breeze tickled his hair. He had on one of those striped shirts she'd seen him wear and the pink and brown made his coffee eyes deep and rich, his dark hair nearly black. And he had one arm up over his head like it was easy for him to be there. With her.

Was it like this for every girl who looked at Cort? she wondered. *Or am I getting fringed around the edges?* The sight of him made it incredibly easy to forgive and forget.

"I have a confession," he said after a time.

"You?"

He looked over, one leg pushing himself into a lazy swing. "Yeah."

"You don't owe me anything."

I do if this is going where I want it to, he thought. She was gorgeous with her legs pulled up to her chest, her long, dark hair messy around her face from the breeze. She looked thrown together, and Cort liked that she didn't fuss about herself.

"When I ran into you on the street. It wasn't an accident."

"It wasn't?" she laughed. "What, were you really following me?"

"Yeah."

"Why?"

"I was making sure of something."

Rachel's eyes narrowed. "That I wasn't a prostitute?"

"Uh," words left him. "How? I—"

128

"That's an old rumor Bree's been trying to pass around for a long time. She whips it out every now and then."

"And you don't care?"

Rachel shrugged. Her heart pinched with his honest announcement, even though she was pretending it hadn't.

"I can't even say the word."

"Good."

"I wanted to see for myself."

"So you believed her."

"No. I wanted to know for myself that she was lying."

"I'll believe that. But didn't you think for one second how absurd it was? I mean, if we lived in Hollywood maybe but, dude, we're in Pleasant View. Campfire Girls sell cookies here, you know?"

Cort laughed. "I saw you walking and followed you to Countryside Manor."

Rachel sat erect. "You did?"

"I heard you reading." His foot stopped rocking the hammock. "You were awesome."

She sat back, not sure if she should be flattered or annoyed. "I've never been followed before."

"Then it was a first for both of us."

"Oh, come on. I've seen girls tripping themselves behind you."

He sat up. "You're the one with the pack."

"I told you, they're just friends."

"Yeah, right."

Across the expanse of the deck, their eyes locked. A wind chime played in the air creating a mystic melody. Cort patted the emptiness beside him.

Rachel stood and crossed, looking down at him. She knew what he wanted; she just wasn't ready to give it to him. "We cleared this up. Good."

His big brown eyes searched her face, heating her skin.

"You're gorgeous," he murmured.

His lazy tone made her smile, but she wouldn't share the hammock with him—this was a practiced move for him, she was sure. Even though he was wracking up scores on his side like crazy, the hammock was dangerous too soon.

"You say that to all the girls when you're sitting on a hammock, right?"

The dreamy intensity on his face changed. His jaw squared. He stood, looked down at her as if he wasn't sure he should touch her or push her away.

"You ever going to cut me a break?" His voice was hard.

She blew it. But she didn't want to be a victim of a trite cliché. "Maybe."

He let out a huff. "Maybe?" Then he looked off for a moment. "You ever going to give me an answer besides, *maybe?*"

She lifted her shoulders, feeling the weight of ruining what had promised to be a nice night. Her mind scrambled with how to save it. His dark eyes flecked with disappointment but it wasn't because he was leaving without getting something from her. She'd hurt his trust.

"See ya, around, Rachel." He avoided touching her and started off the deck.

Pride kept her from stopping him. He'd believed Bree or

he wouldn't have followed her. That was a strike against him, even if he had said otherwise. This was probably better, she thought and she crossed back to the hammock, still swinging from him. She lowered herself where he'd sat. The loopy fabric was still warm from his body.

THIRTEEN

On his break, Cort met the guys at Minerva's for drinks. The sun was high overhead. They sat under the shade of a purple and green umbrella.

"Ah." Cort sat back in his chair, sipped from a steaming latte. "This is the life."

Chad and Eric laughed. "It may be for you," Eric told him.

"Yeah, women everywhere. How did you get so freakin' lucky?"

Cort shrugged a shoulder. "Desperation."

"See," Chad said, "I don't think I could rub girls' feet all day."

"I don't think I could rub girls' feet *any* day," Ben bristled. "My mom has corns the size of knuckles on her toes and if all girls' feet are like that then no way."

"Jenn has hot feet," John said. The guys all snickered.

"Yeah, yeah."

John grinned at Cort. "I may need some massage pointers, dude."

Cort couldn't stop smiling. "You guys are missing the point. There's psychology behind it." He leaned forward, as if going to tell a secret and the boys followed suit. "Look at it this way. You're sitting there and the room is filled with women—hot, gorgeous women of all ages, and they are waiting in line for you to take their hands and—"He demonstrated by grabbing Chad's hand and slowly massaging his fingers. The guys watched, mesmerized.

"Then you take their feet, the grossest part of anybody's body, right? And you're, like, caressing them with fruity smelling cream and oil. I'm telling you, females are putty in your hands."

Eric sat back, shaking his head. "It could be kind of cool, I guess."

"There are worse things than feet," Chad agreed, looking at his hands with new admiration.

But Ben shook his head. "Not when they look like unicorns."

Eric shoved him. "Unicorns are fairy tale horse things, dude."

"And you gotta do girls like Bree," John pointed out. "She'd have hooves—like Satan."

The boys roared with laughter. Minerva came out carrying a flat basket lined with a colorful plaid napkin. Small scones were laid neatly inside. "You boys want to try some of these cranberry orange scones?" She set the basket on the table. "On the house, Cort. With all the business I've gotten since you started working at Miss Chachi's, I owe you."

Cort plucked one from the basket. "Thanks, Minerva. They look great."

"This your break?" she asked.

"Yeah. And I forgot lunch, so this is awesome."

"Well, then, enjoy." The door to her shop jingled when she went back inside.

"Man," John said. "You're hot property down here."

Cort chewed the dense, soft scone. "I'm doing what I can to further enterprise in our fair town."

"Yeah right," Chad slugged his shoulder. "You're doing what you can to fill your wallet and find babes. What's up with you and that Rachel chick?"

Cort frowned as he chewed. He hadn't thought of Rachel in at least an hour and had been glad for it. "Nothing."

After last night, he wasn't sure he wanted to prove he was different than every other jock out there anymore. She seemed to challenge everything he did.

"Hey, Rachel's cool," John took a drink. "You should go for it."

"Bree says—"

"Bree's a two-faced liar," Cort snapped at Ben and chewed his last bite furiously. "She's a viper."

"A hot viper, though," Ben said.

"Not if you know her." Cort brushed the crumbs from his hands. "That's one thing this job has done is open my eyes."

"I'll bet she has hot feet, even," Ben mused, adjusting his baseball cap backwards.

"You'd have to be a retard to like Bree," Cort said in all seriousness. "I've seen her in action and she fires bullets from that mouth of hers."

Ben looked over Cort's shoulder, down the street to the

front of the salon where women came and went with the regularity of water down stream. "Who needs to talk when you've got a bod like that?"

"You're not hearing me," Cort persisted. "She'd massacre you."

"So I wear protective armor." Ben stood, stretched. Cort squinted up at him.

"You're serious about this?"

Ben shrugged. "Prom's coming."

The boys snickered and rose to their feet. Cort took one last drink from his cup then set it down on the table. "There are easier ways to get action on prom night, dude. And still come out alive."

"I want a sure thing this time." Ben started toward the salon. "I'm sick of waiting."

Nobody said anything. Cort was just as anxious as the next guy, but he wanted something special, something different. And where a lot of guys emphasized what happened after prom, he was too practical now, after working so hard for his money, to waste hundreds of dollars on a one night thing with somebody disposable.

"You going to go?" Eric asked him.

"Maybe." Cort thought again of Rachel. If he asked her she'd probably say "maybe" and drive him crazy. "You guys want to come in for a cuticle treatment?"

They playfully slugged at him and soon the boys were jostling with each other in front of the salon until Miss Chachi came out with her hands on her hips and a frown on her face.

"Break over now, Cort," she snapped.

"Later, dudes." Cort wrestled free of his grappling friends. Ben stuck his hands in his pockets, a smile of mischief still on his face.

"Forget Bree, man," Cort told him as he stood in the door of the salon.

But Ben only grinned.

Bree sat like a queen perched on the big, fat pedicure chair. She wore a short skirt and tight tee. Her long, bare legs extended as if someone had artfully posed them to look their very best. Her feet were soaking.

She was waiting for him.

Cort strolled to the back of the salon, trying to remember how despicable she was as those long, brown legs screamed for notice. Miss Chachi was keeping her company and turned to him, her black eyes narrowed. "Miss Bree wait long for you, Cort."

He shot Bree a careless shrug. "Her feet needed it."

Bree's mouth dropped. Miss Chachi grabbed a hunk of his sleeve and tugged him through the hanging beads and into the narrow, dark hall.

"Chill, chill," he told her.

"I not chill anything. I kick you out if you talk like that again to client." Her finger wagged under his nose. "Now I 'cpect apology."

"Okay, I'm sorry," he said.

She shook from head to toe, like a tremor of frustration rumbled through her. "Not me—her!"

Cort followed her pointed finger with his gaze, looked

through the beads that hung in the doorway. Bree.

"No way," he said. "I won't do it."

"You will or you lose job this minute."

Cort looked at the little lady in front of him. She was a teapot ready to blow. All that was missing was steam coming out of the top of her head. He needed the money and he kind of liked the job, even with her volatile personality, even with the long hours and the headaches of girls like Bree. Pride lodged in his throat. He had no choice if he wanted to keep his wallet fat.

He pushed aside the beads and strode to Bree's chair. She looked up and smiled. "Hello, Cortie."

"I'm sorry," he said between teeth.

"Oh, no problem." She crossed her legs and they shimmered in the light.

Miss Chachi gave him a little shove to sit. Cort looked around for the stool but Bree pointed to where Shaylee sat. "On your knees, Cortie."

Cort looked at Miss Chachi. As if she'd do anything to upset the princess, he thought dismally and kneeled down.

When Miss Chachi finally went up front, he glared at Bree. Primly she lifted a leg, aiming her foot his way. He resisted the temptation to look at where that left her short skirt and took her foot in his hands.

When he started the massage, her head fell back and she let out a low moan. Cort glanced around. "Mmm," Bree said. "Nobody has the touch like you do."

"Is that why you come in here twice a week? Or does Daddy pay for whatever you want?" he hissed.

"Both," she answered without a pinch of guilt. "Girls, you really should try Cort out. He's amazing."

Cort glanced at Shaylee and Megan who looked at him blankly.

"Of course," Bree went on, her eyes closed, head resting back. "I found him first."

"It's okay," Shaylee said quickly. "I kind of like Tiaki anyway."

Megan nodded. "And Misu's fine for me."

"Then I get him all to myself." Bree peered at him. "Lucky me."

Cort rolled his eyes.

"I don't need to work," Bree went on. "But if I did, I think this would be a cool place. You like it here?"

He shrugged, and moved on to her other foot.

"How come you talk to your other clients and not to me?" Bree asked.

"I talk to you."

"You'll get better tips."

"I listen mostly. Some girls don't want to talk."

Bree nodded. "They just want to relax. Because it feels so good. Mmm."

Her tone caused an unwanted trembling somewhere inside of him. He swallowed a hard knot in his throat and focused on her feet.

"You guys go get me a drink from that Minerva's place," Bree commanded.

As if they were robots programmed to respond, Shaylee and Megan got up and left. Bree's sharp gaze pinned Cort as he rubbed her calf. "You know what?"

He tried to stay focused. But her smooth leg was in his hands. Her calf, slick with oil, was moving under his fingers, sleek and wet.

"I think we should go to prom together."

He stopped the massage for a moment, forced to regroup. "Why?"

"Why not?"

"We're not together."

"But we're friends."

"We *were* friends."

Bree leaned close, looked around to make sure no one was listening. "We still are. What's wrong with you?"

Absently, Cort took her leg in long, slow strokes. "Nothing. But I might ask someone else."

Bree sat back. Her thumb went between her teeth and she started biting.

"That's why your white tip is always gone on that thumb," he pointed out.

As if she hadn't heard him, she kept chewing nervously. "It's our last prom, Cort. I really want us to go together."

"There are tons of guys who would go with you Bree. Ask one of them."

"I don't want them, I want you."

He looked at her for a moment. Months ago, that statement would have blown him away. But he knew her too well now and could never look at her without seeing beyond the synthetic veneer.

Gently he set her leg back on the foot rest. "I can't say

yes." He oiled his hands and took her other leg.

She leaned close. "What? You want me to beg? Okay. For you I will."

"I didn't ask you to. I just said no."

"It's that Rachel chick isn't it?" She glared at him with mean in her eyes. He only looked at her for a second; afraid his face might give his heart away. "What do you see in her, anyway? I'm so much cuter. Besides, I told you, she's a—"

"She's not." Unconsciously, he squeezed her leg.

"Ouch!"

"Sorry, sorry."

"Be careful. My skin's very delicate."

Cort tried not to laugh. When he rolled his eyes, the gesture infuriated Bree more. "This is your last chance," she told him.

"I wouldn't go to the bathroom with you, Bree, let alone prom."

She slapped him.

For a second, he was so stunned, he didn't move. He was frozen, his face turned to the room for all to see as it bled red with color. Then he reached up and touched his jaw, as if he still couldn't believe she'd hit him.

"You deserved it." Bree hissed and scrambled off the chair, gathering her things. "You're a loser. A virgin and a loser." She leaned over so that she was close to his face. "And you're going to lose your job. I just hope she's worth it."

Bree marched to the front. Her voice pitched like nails on glass. Miss Chachi nodded, looked at him, and nodded some more. Then Bree stormed out.

FOURTEEN

Cort didn't lose his job but Miss Chachi once again dragged him back behind the dangling beads and chewed him out. She wanted him to apologize to Bree but he flatly refused. Even after she told him how much revenue Bree brought in monthly, he still refused.

He pointed out that Bree didn't deserve anything after slapping him. He could refuse her his services forever more.

Miss Chachi tried to talk him into being reasonable and it was then Cort knew he carried more cards in Miss Chachi's deck then he realized. He thought about it the next day as he walked to Miss Tingey's class in a rare moment of being alone.

Then Bree appeared out of nowhere. He didn't expect her to talk to him ever again, let alone walk alongside of him.

"I want you to know I've forgotten about how rude you were yesterday," Bree started sweetly.

"Too bad." He kept walking. "I was hoping you'd stay away from me."

"I could never do that, Cortie. We're too good of friends."

He snickered, turned the corner and took the stairs up to Miss Tingey's classroom.

"Besides." She was still at his elbow. "I thought maybe I

should apologize for slapping you."

He stopped and looked at her. It was the first time he'd ever heard her say she was sorry for anything. He tried to find the lie in her eyes.

She stood close, so her body brushed his.

"Forgive me?"

"We're still not going to prom," he said.

"Oh, that's cool. I just wanted you to know I'd never hurt you." She touched the side of his face. "Did it hurt?"

He was confused by this repentant, nicer Bree. Something wasn't right. "No," he lied. He went up the stairs to class, relieved she didn't follow. Eyes desperate for something normal searched for his friends as he entered Miss Tingey's class. He looked for Rachel. She was already seated and she didn't bother to look up at him.

Miss Tingey wrote the day's journal entry on the board. Contention—how it makes us stronger. *Is that what it does?* Contention made him feel like he'd swallowed a bag of ticking explosives.

He buried his head in crossed arms and let out a sigh. What was Bree's problem? She'd turned into this monster he didn't want to have anything more to do with. But the more he pushed her away, the stronger she came on.

He couldn't understand why she was doing it. They'd known each other for years, been friends once. She still thought they were friends. But his perception of friends and friendship had changed. Friends didn't try to manipulate each other.

And what about Rachel? She'd all but given him the

brush off the other night. He looked at her, felt a jab that she wasn't even looking at him.

He had to figure this out somehow.

He sat up, rubbed his hands down his face, picked up his pen and started writing.

The room echoed with the sound of frantic scratching as students wrote. Rachel snuck glances across the room at Cort. His face was twisted. Was he upset? Could she help that the sight bothered her? For all she knew, he was troubled because of her.

She tried to think herself out of it. He was mad at her, she figured that much, after being so harsh that night he'd come over to talk. *Don't flatter yourself, honey. It's not like you two had anything.*

She was still trying to decide if she liked that. What she did like was that he went out of his way to impress her. Cort Davies tried to change her mind about jocks. For however long it lasted, was a very cool thing.

Concentrating on the assignment, she decided to push thoughts of Cort away—for her own good.

Sure, contention makes you have a tougher, thicker skin and every teenager needs that just to make it through. I don't mind it either. With every situation I learn new ways to navigate. When I finally get out of school and into real life, I'll have a compass and some skin that can't be penetrated with insignificant darts from losers like those who give us grief in high school.

"Who wants to share?" Miss Tingey asked.

Cort raised his hand and she nodded at him. Rachel's nerves ripened as she waited for him to speak.

"Contention sucks," Cort started. The class agreed. "If it makes us stronger, I guess we need it. But how much is enough? Does the more we have mean we'll be that much stronger? If it does, I should say, bring it on. But I hate it at the same time. Am I the only one that feels this way?"

"Anybody else feel overwhelmed by contention?" Miss Tingey asked.

"I think it overwhelms when you can't figure out what to do about it," Rachel suggested.

Cort shot her a look. "You'd just shrug it off with a maybe."

"Maybe," Rachel said, trying to keep her voice steady. "Sometimes that's what you need to do because some things aren't worth it. But when something is worth it, you take it head on, no matter how bad it is or how bad you think it might get."

"Even when somebody's screwing you over?" Cort's tone rose.

Rachel looked around. Did he think she was screwing him over? She was being careful, taking it slow. "Maybe you don't know what's really happening," she offered.

"Oh, I know what's happening," he said and didn't look at her again. It took every bit of courage she had inside not to let his mood drive her in the opposite direction.

Rachel wasn't sure what made her approach him at the end of class. Maybe it was the hope that whatever friendship had started to bud wouldn't wither and die.

"You okay?" She stood by his desk as class filed out.

He looked up. Pleasure tried to break on his face but

whatever was bugging him, smothered it. "Yeah."

They walked down the hall together.

"Did I say something to make you mad the other night?" she finally asked.

"I just got the impression you didn't want me there anymore."

"Because I didn't sit with you on the hammock?"

He smiled. "Maybe."

Rachel laughed and was glad when he did too. "Okay, so I messed up. Sorry about that."

"Forgiven." He stopped at the top of the stairs. Suddenly, he reached for her hand. His was warm, strong, as he lifted hers and looked at her nails.

"They look good," he said.

"No air bubbles."

"I was hoping you'd broken one or one was lifting."

He ran his thumb across her knuckles and she almost lost her train of thought. "Uh. They're still perfect. I can come into the salon anyway."

Gently he let her hand go. "I have some clients who come in for a hand massage."

"Seriously?"

He nodded and started down the stairs. "But you could so easily do that yourself." She stopped suddenly. "Hey, I have an idea."

"What?"

"Would you consider coming with me to Countryside Manor and giving hand massages?"

"Sure." She looked so genuinely pleased, pleasure seeped

into him. He couldn't wait to spend more time with her. "When?"

"Tomorrow night. Will you be able to get off work?"

"I didn't think of that." But he'd do whatever it took. "I'll be there."

"Meet me at six."

"I'll pick you up?" He offered as they parted in the hall.

"Okay."

FIFTEEN

Rachel stood in front of her mirror with a frown working its way onto her face. She never thought much about what she wore to Countryside Manor. With Cort picking her up, she mused over her jeans and long-sleeved black tee.

Maybe black is too goth. But then she looked great in the color. In fact, color was telling. Guys that liked her in black were often the ones she clicked with.

She slipped the black tee on.

She'd never worn perfume to Countryside and looked now at her assortment of bottles sitting on the dresser. Nothing was more enticing than a guy who smelled good. She'd had guys tell her they liked her perfume but she had yet to hear the words from Cort. She would never give up a scent—even for a guy.

She sprayed some at her throat, her wrists.

Her hair hung straight after a painstaking hour with the flat iron. Some guys liked curls. Some liked hair up. She wouldn't ruin a perfectly good straightening job by pulling it up and leaving rubber band or claw marks in it.

She left her hair down.

On her dresser, the script she was going to read: Tennessee Williams' *Streetcar Named Desire*, waited. She'd borrowed the play from Jennifer. She'd get through half of it tonight, but that was okay. They could finish it next time.

She waited for Cort downstairs, pacing in front of the mirror her mother had in the entry, an antique they'd picked up in Paris one year. She liked the soft, fuzzy way the glass made her look.

Her heart started when the doorbell rang. Cort looked amazing in dark jeans and a bulky grey, crew-neck sweater.

When his eyes roamed her from head to toe, she tingled. "You look great," he said.

"Yeah? Thanks. You look nice yourself."

She followed him to his car and he opened her door. "Would you rather drive your car?" he asked.

"No." The last thing she wanted was for him to think she was a snob. When he started the car, Click Five blasted from the speakers. *Another point.*

"I love this CD," she said.

"Me too."

"So what are you reading tonight?"

"Streetcar."

"Tennessee Williams?"

"You know him?"

"Not personally. He died a long time ago."

"You know what I mean."

He grinned at her. "Yeah, I do. What gave you the idea to do this? To go there and read to them?"

"I went there once for a service project with this girl's group I belonged to. We hung out with them, pushed them around in their wheel chairs and stuff. I saw this lady reading to one of the older people and later, I remembered thinking that could be a nice thing."

He glanced over as he drove. "You're awesome."

She shrugged.

"Like how you wear black all the time."

"It's just a color I like."

"I like that you wear what you want even if everybody else is into something different."

"Wait," she said teasingly. "Are you trying to tell me something?"

"You look hot in it."

She hoped she wasn't blushing, but her cheeks felt like toasty mittens.

They pulled up in front of the Manor and he surprised her by reaching over her body and holding her door in place. His firm body pressed against her, his face inched near. She felt his breath, the black flecks of color in his eyes sparkled.

"Don't move," he said.

She couldn't if she wanted to. She liked the feel of him pressing into her, even if it only lasted for a second. He hopped out and opened her door before she could smile.

"Thanks," she said. "I've never had a guy do that before. Except my dad."

He locked the car with the press of a remote. He sent her that all-American grin and she wanted to melt. Or take a picture. At that moment she would never forget the way he looked.

"I come early most nights because my friends here go to bed around eight or eight-thirty," she told him.

He pulled open the front door of the Manor. "Man, I haven't gone to bed that early since I was eight."

"Me either," she laughed. "What's funny is when one or two of them fall asleep while I'm reading."

"Must be that sexy voice of yours," he said.

She glanced away, knowing she was red. They waved at Charity, sitting behind the front desk and Cort followed Rachel into the gathering room.

The group was the same, and they were all in a semi-circle, waiting for her.

She waved and smiled and she crossed the floor to them.

Cort was uncomfortable as a mouse in a room full of traps. Unlike Rachel, he'd never had any experience with older people other than the very occasional visit with his out-of-state grandparents. His hands sweat, his armpits drenched.

Rachel kissed each of their cheeks like the gesture was nothing. Touched them as if they weren't so old they looked like they might crack. That was it, he thought, they all looked so fragile. It was frightening.

Suddenly they all looked at him.

Rachel waved him over and he approached with feigned courage. Heck, he could fake this, right?

Rachel introduced each one. He'd never remember their names. He'd never heard of a woman named Mannie before. But she examined him with eyes amazingly bright, even surrounded by wrinkles like walnut shells.

"We've seen you before," Mannie told him, her critical eye checking him out.

"Oh, yeah?"

"At Kippers Fish and Chips." Lily smiled warmly at him. "I remember. Such a handsome young man."

Mannie appeared undecided. "That doesn't mean anything, Lily. No one knows better than we do that beauty is only skin deep."

"Leave the poor boy alone," Martin scowled. "He's here to give you gals hand massages. Stop your bickering or he'll leave, won't you young sir?"

Totally blasted by what was happening around him, Cort rocked back on his heels with a shrug.

"Massages?" Lily nearly whispered. Her frail hand went to her mouth, covering a smile. "Oh, my."

Rachel pulled a chair over for Cort and placed it in front of Priscilla, a woman who only occasionally sat in on the readings. She had jet black hair and sharp features like a witch.

"Is it okay if he starts with you, Priscilla?"

Priscilla nodded. "I need it most." She held out two hands that looked like they'd spent the last fifty years submerged in water.

Cort pulled the small tube of herbal scented oil he'd brought out of his pants pocket, sat down and tried to steady his hands. It felt like every eye in the room was on him. He looked up. Sure enough, heads strained from every corner to see. And those sitting in the semi-circle stared.

He didn't know if he should touch the woman. Something about it seemed wrong. But Rachel started reading and he was keenly aware that, even with the exciting story, he was the focus and would be until they saw what he was going to do.

He took one of Priscilla's hands and, finding it amazingly warm, gently began a slow massage. "Tell me if I'm being too rough," he told her.

The blackness of her eyes reminded him of a crow. He was scared of her. Forget that she was under a hundred pounds, bony as a skeleton. She looked like the grim reaper's wife.

"You do this for a living?" she asked, even though Rachel was in the middle of reading.

"Shhh!" Martin stuck his gnarled finger to his lips.

Cort nodded. Priscilla's onyx eyes pinned him like thumbtacks to a wall.

"How old are you?" Priscilla blurted.

Cort moved a little closer so he could speak softly and not interrupt Rachel's reading. "Seventeen."

"You're a baby!"

"Would you keep it down?" Martin scowled.

Rachel cleared her throat. "Should we take a break?"

"Are you a masseuse?" Priscilla continued.

"Uh. I'm not."

Priscilla yanked her hand free. "Then why are you giving me a massage?"

"Oh, for Pete's sake." Martin wheeled himself over. "He's a friend of Rachel's, 'Cilla."

"That doesn't answer my question about why he's massaging my hand."

"I don't have to—"Cort started.

"I wasn't complaining." Priscilla stuck her hand back out

at him. "Just wondering."

"Well quit wondering so we can listen." Martin turned himself to face Rachel and shook his head.

Rachel started reading again. Cort's clothes dampened with perspiration. His hands were clammy and slick, mixing with the oil. He hoped Priscilla couldn't tell he was ready to die right there on the spot he was so uncomfortable—thanks to her.

"Oh, I like this," Lily gushed, her hands pressed at her chest as if in prayer. "Mr. Williams is a very good writer."

"A famous one," Martin told her. "Didn't you ever see Marlon Brando in the film?"

"Oh, heavens yes," Lily said. "He was beautiful."

"A man if I ever saw one," Priscilla piped out of nowhere, staring intently at Cort. He sent her a fast smile. "You're a boy yet."

"Oh." Cort laughed. He hoped he wasn't offending the older woman.

"Shall I continue?" Rachel asked.

"Oh, do lovey." Mannie nodded. "Now everyone hush."

Rachel started again, her deep voice taking on the character of tormented Stella. Cort forgot he was doing something he had seriously doubted he could do when he'd first walked into the room.

He moved from Priscilla to Mannie and though Priscilla didn't thank him, she stared at her hands and he thought she looked more relaxed and happy.

Mannie gave his hands a squeeze and smiled at him when he finished.

Something about Lily made Cort's heart squeeze. Her wispy grey hair, pulled back and knotted at the back of her fragile head accentuated her big blue eyes—eyes that looked on the verge of tears. She'd been pretty once, he guessed, then felt guilty thinking that. She was still pretty, just aged.

When he took her hands, she lit up like an ivory candle, pulling him close so she could whisper, "This is so lovely." She patted the side of his face.

Carefully, he rubbed each of her fingers, feeling large knobs of arthritis. He watched her face for signs he was causing her any discomfort but she just smiled, her blue eyes twinkling like water under the sun.

When Rachel finished reading, Martin applauded. "Wonderful. Now that's what I call a story."

"All stories are stories, Martin," Mannie scoffed.

"But not all stories are equal."

Rachel closed the script. "We'll finish next time. Did everyone enjoy the massages?"

Nods and murmurs of agreement followed.

"What a lovely boy," Lily told Cort, watching him massage her hands.

Cort didn't know what to say. He'd never been called lovely before. "You and our lovey make such a beautiful couple."

"We're not a couple," Rachel said quickly. They all looked at her as if she'd just profaned. Then they looked at Cort who started to sweat again.

"Only because she won't let me be her man," he joked.

Instantly, all faces looked to Rachel. She wanted to laugh,

but she tried to figure out what to say. Cort was playing, that's all. So she did too. "I'm still deciding if I want a man."

"Of course you want a man," Priscilla snapped. "Look at him. He's still a boy. Find a man."

Cort and Rachel looked at each other over amused grins.

"And she's still a girl," Mannie pointed out.

"She's twenty-seven!" Priscilla exclaimed.

"I'm seventeen," Rachel corrected.

"You look twenty-seven." With that Priscilla rose from her chair. "But you'll do what you want. That's what all teenagers do." She waved her hand dismissively at Rachel and the group before turning and starting across to the window.

SIXTEEN

Even with spring whispering at the door, the night air was cold. Trees danced, bushes shuffled in the wind, and Cort stuffed his hands in his pockets, wishing he'd thought to bring a coat.

Rachel clutched the script to her chest. Her hair scattered around her face from the breeze, giving Cort the urge to reach over and move a strand caught on her clear lip gloss.

"You cold?" he asked as they headed to his car.

"A little but—" She stopped the instant his arm wrapped around her shoulder.

"Is this okay?" He looked at her through tentative eyes.

She wouldn't have shrugged his arm off for a thousand blankets. "Sure."

"I don't know." He slowed their walk a little. "With you I want to ask permission."

"Why?"

"I don't know." At the car, he didn't take his arm away. And he didn't open the door. He slid her around so she faced him and rested his hands on her shoulders. "You're not like anyone else I know."

Neither are you, she thought but didn't say. He'd

probably heard that hundreds of times from hundreds of girls. "That can't be the first time you've said that."

His eyes narrowed. "You don't give me much of a chance, Rache."

"I'm sorry." She looked away. "It's just that this is hard for me."

"What's hard?"

"This—all of this."

"You and me?"

She nodded. "We're so different but here you are."

His hands fell from her shoulders. "How are we different?"

"I don't know, we just are." The excuse was weak. She couldn't tell him it was hard to believe a guy like him was interested in a girl like her. That stuff like this happened on the Disney channel, not in real life.

"If you think it's about money—"

"No." She shook her head. "No, I don't think that."

"Good." He let out a sharp sigh. "Because that's just stupid."

"You know how you said that with me you feel like you have to ask permission?" she asked. He nodded. "With you, I have to check my pulse."

"Check your pulse?"

"To see if this is real."

He studied her face, drawing his lower lip between his teeth, his beautiful mouth curving into a smile. Then he stepped closer and set his hands on her shoulders again. When his gaze shifted to her mouth her heart skipped.

She closed her eyes. It was too unbelievable that he was going to kiss her but he did. The warm softness of his mouth met hers and every part of her went soft and weak. Her heart sung through her veins. She had to touch him.

She wound her free arm around his neck. Cloudy softness enveloped her, taking her senses into the dark loftiness of the endless sky.

He turned rigid against her, drawing her against the stone length of his body. His hands left her shoulders, slid down her waist.

"Rache." He pulled back and took a breath.

For a moment she was disoriented. "What? Why did you stop?"

After a swallow, he wet his lips. His gaze was tight on her face. "You're cold. I feel it. Let's get in the car." He opened the door.

Confused, she slid into the car wondering if she'd done something wrong.

He got in and looked at the steering wheel, he looked so tense, something was wrong.

She reached over but he shot his dark eyes at her so fast she pulled her hand back like she'd been stung. "What's wrong?" The moment was unlike any she had ever lived through. A kiss she'd never experienced before, one that still flooded her veins.

He brought his lower lip between his teeth—a gesture she thought adorable, making him look innocent and vulnerable. "Did I do something?" she asked.

He shook his head. "The kiss was great." He started the

car.

The kiss was more than great, she thought, a little frustration simmering. But then maybe he'd kissed so many girls that he rated her against the throngs and she didn't have anything more than great to offer. Maybe that was the problem.

He drove in silence, edgy and distracted, until they reached her house. The engine hummed as they sat in the warmth of the car.

"I shouldn't have kissed you," he finally said.

"Why not?"

"I want it to be different with you."

"Isn't it different because it's me?"

"It is. But I should have waited. I'm sorry."

"Waited for what?"

His hands gripped the steering wheel, he shrugged. "I don't know. I just don't want to do anything wrong with you."

"If you're worried about proving you're not like other jocks, don't worry about that anymore." She leaned close and he took immediate notice. "You're not."

"It's not just that," he said. "I don't want anything between us to be like anything I've ever had with somebody else. You're—" He looked at her long and hard. "You're too good for that."

Her heart leapt to her throat and banged there. "Whoa." She sat back, awed and afraid.

"See? Now you're scared."

Amazed is more like it. He so exceeded what she thought he was. "I don't scare that easily."

"Good." Their eyes locked across the car. She wanted to kiss him again, but he didn't make any moves that he wanted the same.

He killed the engine.

"Rache."

"Yes?"

"Would you go to prom with me?"

Rachel's breath skipped, and tied around a knob in her throat. She tried to swallow but couldn't. She wanted to scream, to laugh, to cry. Wrap around him and kiss him again. But she just said, "Yes."

His lips broke into a smile. "Great."

She leaned over and kissed his cheek, taking one last breath of him with her. "Thanks for helping tonight," she whispered against his cheek.

He seemed in a daze after the kiss but he blinked and it was gone. "I'd like to go again, if that's okay with you."

"They'd love it."

"So I can?"

She nodded.

He got out and opened her door for her.

"Just let me know when," she said.

He shut the door and walked alongside her to the porch. Because he kept a fair distance between them, Rachel figured he wasn't going to kiss her again. She respected that. If he wanted things to be different, she'd let him have that. For her, the night was already in another sphere.

When Cort pulled up into the driveway of his house, he was startled to find Lizzie coming at him at a full run, waving her arms frantically above her head. He rolled the window down to talk but she ran to the passenger side.

"What the—" He unlocked the door so she could climb in.

Out of breath, she slammed the door, gasping.

"What's wrong?" His heart hammered. "Is Mom okay?"

She nodded, still gulping air. "Go," she spit out, "as fast as you can. Drive us to Taco Bell."

Cort rolled his eyes, felt a smile bloom. He backed the car down the drive. "Why? Mom been in the kitchen all day?"

"Yes." Lizzie's breath slowly steadied. "And it smells like fermenting shoes. I'm telling you, I can't take another day of it. Do you know I've lost five pounds? Look at me, I'm practically anorexic."

"I thought girls could never be too rich or too thin."

Lizzie cocked her head. "Where've you been all night?"

He glanced at the car clock. "It's only nine."

"Still."

"I was helping out a friend."

"Hmm."

"Don't try to read something into it. You'll never know."

Lizzie stuck both of her tennis-shoed feet on the dashboard. "Rachel Baxter."

"How did you—" He reached out to snag her but she inched back with a taunting laugh.

"You left your computer on with Facebook open—Duh. Mom could have read it."

"Oh, but it's better you did?"

"Way. I closed it for you by the way. After I sent her a

long, juicy, message signed by you."

He glared at her. "You're dead."

She wiggled her feet to the beat of the music. "She's a cool girl, Rachel. Go for it."

"Like I'd listen to you."

"Except when it comes to your stomach."

They drove along State Street and Cort checked out cars and drivers out of habit, but it was Rachel's car he wished he saw. Scamming and driving are so juvenile, he thought now. He kept his eyes on the road.

He pulled into the drive-thru and they ordered then sat and relished their tacos and burritos.

The drive home was filled with sighs of contentment.

"Now that was food," Lizzie said. "I'll be glad when Mom's off this health thing. Thankfully the holidays are long gone. Can you see it? Tofu turkey?" She stretched her arms out on the seat and felt something, lifted it to the light.

"What's this?"

Cort looked over. His massage lotion. He reached out to snatch it but she yanked it back.

"Massage elixir?" she shrieked. "What are you doing with this?"

"I use it at work."

"Oh, yeah, I bet. You do nails, Cort. Massages are something else all together."

"Hand massages," he emphasized and reached again for the tube but she refused to relinquish it.

"I want one."

He bristled. "Forget it."

"Come on, I'm your sister."

"Exactly."

"So you only give massages to girls you're sexually attracted to?"

Cort thought of the old women he'd given massages to just hours ago. "No, but—"

"Then you give me one and I'll critique it, tell you how well you do. Stuff like that."

He made another grab for it. "I don't need your critique. Girls love it. Now give me—"

"I want one or I tell Mom I found love elixir in your car."

"It's not love elixir!"

"Looks pretty slick to me."

"Give me the tube!"

Her eyes danced with mischief. "Not until—"

"Fine, fine! Okay! You can have your freaking massage."

"I'm very discerning, you'll see. What were you doing with love elixir tonight, huh? Or should I cover my ears."

"You are so way off. I was helping Rachel out."

She let out a snort. "Uh-huh."

"It wasn't like that. She's not like that."

"And you aren't? Ha!"

"You don't know anything."

"I know you're a hormone nightmare like most teenaged boys. So I imagine this little bottle comes in quite handy."

"Cut it out, where's your head? In the toilet?" Cort enjoyed the shock in her eyes. "Seriously, Liz, guys don't like girls who talk with a lot of innuendo or sleaze. Cut it out."

She was silent for a moment, turning the tube in her

fingers. He glanced over, softened his voice. "If you can critique me, I can do the same, right?"

She shrugged but still didn't say anything.

They walked into the house and Cort's gag reflex kicked in. Lizzie was right, the place reeked of sour, stinky shoes. "What the—"

"It's dinner." Their mother was in her usual blue suit but had a white apron tied around her waist. She waved them over as she pulled something oatmeal colored and squiggly-textured from the oven. "Ah," she said, setting the odd meal on the burners with a smile. "Macrobiotic meatloaf," she announced.

Lizzie pinched her nose. "I thought meat, by definition, was off the macrobiotic list."

"It is, but for the sake of identification they still call the recipe that. Looks good, doesn't it?"

Cort and Lizzie exchanged horrified glances. Cort made a b-line for the stairway.

"Cort?"

"I already ate."

"When? Where?"

"Uh, just a few minutes ago."

She marched over to him. "Open up."

"Mom."

"Open up, Cort." Reluctantly he opened his mouth and she leaned close for a sniff. "Lizzie?"

Lizzie shook her head, backing toward the stairs. "I ate what he ate. Ground me, beat me, brand me—whatever, but I am not eating that."

"Quit the courtroom drama." Her mother went back to the meatloaf and looked at it. "It disappoints me when you two cheat. Especially after I make the effort to cook us a bonding dinner."

Cort felt a stab of guilt. He knew how hard it was to earn money, how long the hours. His mother worked hard every day, and the disappointment on her face bothered him.

"We can eat it tomorrow night," he offered.

She looked over. "That would almost work but the point of fresh eating is to eat when it's fresh. No." She dug herself a portion that wiggled as it set on the plate. "I'll eat it. I'll save you two the obvious torture I can see it will cause you to partake."

Lizzie let out a "Phew."

"Want me to sit with you?" Cort asked.

"Thanks, but I have paperwork."

He nodded before taking the stairs up with Lizzie behind him.

Cort and Lizzie sat in front of his computer. Cort was half hoping Rachel would send him a message. He'd kissed her. Just thinking about it sent his blood into a spin. It was the hottest kiss ever. She had great lips, lips he'd stared at and wondered about for eons.

They hadn't disappointed.

But what a retard you are thinking about them like they're body parts, Davies.

Lizzie's hands were out, ready. Giving her a massage would kill any warm, lingering feelings he enjoyed for Rachel, that was a given.

"Let's get this over with," he muttered.

"Do you talk mean to all your clients?"

He took her hands. "I wasn't talking mean."

"You had a tone."

"Just shut up and let me do this."

"Clue one. Never say shut up to a client."

He pinched his lips, tried patience. Squirting lotion into his palms, he warmed the cream before taking her right hand.

"Warming—nice touch," Lizzie observed. She watched as his thumbs and fingers worked her palm and the back of her hand. "Pretty good."

Cort's thoughts drifted back to Rachel and he glanced again at the computer screen. That kiss was like a tidal wave. Had almost washed his restraint right out of him. He could have taken her along, that's why he stopped. There were girls and there were girls, and then there was that special one who deserved something else. That was Rachel.

"Hello?" Lizzie said. "You've like made my palm into putty."

"Oh." He looked at her hand, moved onto her fingers. "Sorry."

"Thinking about Rachel?"

He looked at her blankly, "Maybe," and smiled.

"What's so funny?"

"It's just what she always says."

"You're right. I have heard her say that a lot. Pretty evasive. *Maybe* she doesn't want to commit?"

"We're not committing to anything. But I did ask her to prom."

"She said yes? Or was it *maybe*?"

He smiled, took long, dragging strokes down each finger. "She said yes."

"Wow. That—whoa. That feels great. Who taught you how to do this?"

He lifted a shoulder, set her hand gently on her lap. "I watched the girls at the salon." He squeezed some lotion into his palm again and picked up her other hand. "It's simple."

"It's totally relaxing."

"Endorphins are released into the blood stream when—"

"Don't ruin it for me. You done this to her yet?"

"Yeah."

A smile played on Lizzie's lips. "She's not going to be able to resist."

"So, no comments, no corrections?"

Lizzie shook her head. "If a guy I liked did this to me, it'd be over. I'd do whatever he wanted."

Cort's face burned. That would be excellent, if Rachel felt that way.

"Putty in your hands," Lizzie told him.

Then a sickening thought struck him. He glared at Lizzie. "If I ever hear that you've let a guy get on you—"

"Chill. Chill." Lizzie pulled her hand out of his slick one. "You're the only guy I know who works at a nail salon, Cort. I don't think it's the job of choice for most guys."

Lizzie looked at her hands all pink and plump, and she gleamed. "Awesome."

SEVENTEEN

Prom would be her first and her last. Rachel couldn't believe that she was going with Cort. Senior year, and she'd end it with an explosion. Part of her wondered if she'd made the right choice saying yes. But then there really hadn't been a choice—Cort was the only one who'd asked.

The guys would freak. She expected resistance but when she saw Sam, Pete, Chris and Todd in the parking lot waiting for her, she started to feel defensive.

They converged like dogs around a scrap of meat.

"Tell me I didn't hear what I thought I heard," Sam told her.

"You can't seriously be thinking of going to prom with a poster boy like Cort Davies," Pete said.

Todd fumed silently as they walked up the drag toward the school. Rachel waved to Jennifer, just pulling in, in her sunny yellow VW. The distraction would buy her some time. She headed over.

"Rache?" Sam's voice trailed behind her.

"What you heard is true," Rachel tossed over her shoulder. Glad Jennifer got out of her car, she waited, her back to the boys in a message of leave me alone.

The boys mumbled and took off.

"How's it going?" Rachel walked the rest of the parking lot alongside Jennifer.

"Great. Busy."

"I got asked to prom last night," Rachel said.

Jennifer's eyes lit up. "Who?"

"Magic Hands"

"Wow. I've been out of the loop."

"Love will do that to you." The way Jennifer gleamed made Rachel warm inside. "I don't have to ask how you and John are doing."

"He's so awesome," Jennifer's eyes glazed over.

"Yeah, yeah, yeah."

"Like Magic Hands is not just as cool? And he asked you to prom. I'd say you're doing well." Jennifer looked further up the aisle where the boys had gone on ahead. "The guys must be losing it."

Rachel shrugged. "They'll get over it. They'd better get over it."

"So I guess Cort proved his point, not all jocks are created equal?"

Rachel laughed. Jennifer went on to class and Rachel headed to her locker. She stopped. The door was wrapped in brightly flowered wrapping paper with a giant bow, like a present.

Everybody around her slowed, whispered as she spun the dial and opened the door. The moment she did, hundreds of rose buds fell to her feet, a shower of red, white and pink. Inside, ribbon was twisted in spirals, fluffy bows dotted the sides and in the back was a large sign:

I've fallen for you. Senior Prom

"Oh!" Girls around her squealed. Guys walked by and smiled. Rachel scanned the hall, searching for Cort's face and saw him in the crowd, waiting.

The moment their eyes locked, he made his way to her. A flush of heat ran from her head to her toes. He had his hands in his front pockets, his lower lip between his teeth.

He leaned in close. "I wanted to ask you for real."

"This is so cute." She couldn't believe the flowers. The air smelled like a garden.

"Your answer's still the same, isn't it?" The heat of his breath tickled her ear.

"Of course."

"What's this?"

Rachel turned. Bree stood with Shaylee and Megan, all of them wearing looks meant to cover the envy nearly turning their skin green.

"Wow, how totally cute." Bree sent her jealous eyes to Cort. "You did this?"

Cort nodded.

"Lucky girl." Bree turned to Rachel. "Well, congratulations." But the word didn't disguise the loathing in her tone. "You won't be getting any on Prom night with him, though." Bree flipped her hair over her shoulder and glared at Cort. "And *you're* gonna miss what could have been the most memorable night of your life." She stepped close. "You can ask Ben."

Rachel turned her back on Bree. Cort's narrowed eyes

stayed on Bree until she disappeared in the crowd.

"She's unbelievable," he muttered.

"Thanks, Cort. This was so sweet."

His attention diverted, he smiled at Rachel and walked with her to her next class.

"You work today?" she asked.

He nodded. "Why don't you come by? We could get a drink or something on my break."

"Mrs. Meers is giving you breaks now? Maybe I will."

Cort grinned, and his smile drew an involuntary breath from her chest. "Maybe?" he asked. "Maybe someday I'll rate enough not to hear that word every time I ask you something."

"Don't exaggerate." She pushed him playfully. "I said yes to prom, didn't I?"

"Finally. I gotta go," he said, slowly backing away. "Later?"

Rachel smiled. *So this is what it's like.* She'd said goodbye thousands of times to the guys and gone to class, but this goodbye felt like somewhere inside of her tore a little. No maybe about it.

The week dragged by. Rachel was accustomed to being busy, having her mind occupied by school, friends, and creative ambition. Having Cort on the brain was not something she was used to.

Being in a handful of classes together helped but they hadn't talked—one or both of them always surrounded by friends.

It was getting to the point where Rachel thought both

sets of friends was acting strange, converging like sharks every time either one of them was alone; almost as though they didn't want the two of them together.

That was just paranoia.

She had the right to feel it, this was Cort Davies and very few boys rated in his rank at PV high. What girl wouldn't resort to warfare for a chance at him?

She dressed for another reading at Countryside and thought of Brownie and Ticia. Of *Bree*. Until Bree had a date for prom, Ben was at risk from Bree's claws. Ticia's senior year would be ruined, as the hopes she'd held onto for so long were squashed along with her heart.

Bree was the problem.

Rachel would never rest her hopes and dreams on some guy, but Ticia was that way. For a second, Rachel entertained the fantastical idea that one of the guys—Sam, Pete, Chris or Todd might do her a favor and take Bree. But then if Bree was ready to put out on prom night, she sure wasn't ready to offer Bree's services to one of her friends as a token for the favor.

Besides, she had serious doubts any of her guy friends had ever *been* with girls. They'd never talked about it of course, but she figured by the immature way they interacted with her they were likely all scared of most things female.

Why was it so easy to hang with someone when your heart wasn't dangling along? The heart changed everything.

Cort would be there in five minutes and she couldn't wait. When her Facebook message window opened, she thought it was him.

TOD: I know u r going to prom with davies but the guys

172

and i are getting a group together do u want in?

She felt more than a little guilty, knowing Todd wanted to go with her, knowing all the guys felt deserted.

She wouldn't turn him down just yet. Not until she knew for sure whether or not Cort's friends were planning anything. Traditionally, the person asking organized the night date, the day date, and everything that went into the event. To hang with her friends all night would have certain benefits.

RACHEL: we haven't made plans yet. as soon as i know, i'll tell you. thanks for asking.

TOD: i acted like a retard a few days ago. i guess i thought u would go with me to prom, even though i hadn't asked. it's the way u want it, i can tell. that's cool, i guess.

RACHEL: thanks. yeah, it's going to be fun i think. who are u going to ask?

TOD: maria. kno her?

RACHEL: she's a nice girl. go for it. gotta run. later.

Rachel heard her mother's voice mix with the deeper tone of male down stairs. Cort. Rachel sprayed her favorite floral scent at her wrists, chest and the back of her neck and was out the door, her heart fluttering.

* * *

The evening was comfortably familiar, him picking her up in his car, the two of them driving together to Countryside, like they were a team. Or a couple.

Rachel wondered if that was why she couldn't find words

to fill the quiet. Maybe he felt it too. Maybe he didn't like familiarity. Newness was dissolving already. Maybe he had second thoughts about prom, was sorry he'd asked her.

She'd never thought like this before. But then she'd never felt this way about anybody either. "You ready for this?" she started. "Bring your oil?"

He nodded, looked over and smiled. Any doubts she had melted into nothingness. "At least this time I'm not nervous."

"They're not scary."

"They're kinda cool, actually." He'd looked forward to tonight all week. Part of it was finally being with Rachel, but a place inside of him was comfortable with the seniors, too.

"I think Lily likes you."

"She's a nice lady," he said. "There's something about her that's sweet."

"I know. I've never seen her be anything but sweet."

"What do you know about them?"

Rachel lifted a shoulder. "Different stuff. Like Martin never married. That's probably not hard to believe since he's crabby most of the time. Mannie has four children and they come and visit a lot. I've met most of them. Priscilla, the one with the black eyes? She's been there the longest but only recently started coming to readings. For the longest time she'd sit in the corner and just stare at me."

"Seriously?"

Rachel nodded. "I used to get creeped out but I realized it's just the way she looks."

"What about Lily?"

"Lily had one child who died when she was a young girl."

"Sad."

"And her husband died like sixty years ago. She's been a widow ever since."

"Man. Sad."

As expected, their audience was waiting in a semi-circle. Cort's heart jumped a little from the pleasure of seeing the elderly faces light up at their arrival.

He followed Rachel who kissed each one on the cheek and asked them how they were. He shook each fragile hand, glad they all remembered him.

Lily's delicate hand lingered in his for a moment as she looked up, smiling. "Are you going to work some magic with your hands?"

"If that's okay with you."

"That would be delightful."

"What did you bring for us this time, lovey?" Mannie asked. She adjusted a brightly colored knit throw she had across her lap.

"She's going to finish the *Streetcar Named Desire*, of course," Martin snapped. He jerked his head toward Mannie. "She thinks she's something special because one of her daughters knit her that blanket."

Mannie gleamed. "I am something special. Look what my daughter did for me. Isn't it beautiful?"

"It is." Rachel lifted a corner and fingered the tight craftsmanship."

"My Brigitta's been knitting since she was a teenager. I taught her myself when my hands were good."

"It's very nice," Cort added. Martin made a huff of

disproval and looked away.

"How are you today, Priscilla?" Cort crossed to her and she stared up.

"Lousy."

"Oh…sorry."

"Your hand massage will be the highlight of my week. How's that for you?"

"In that case maybe I should save you for last."

"Hell with that!" Priscilla snapped and stuck out her hands. "You can start with me."

Cort squelched a laugh. He dragged a folding chair over in front of her and sat.

"Shall I start?" Rachel asked.

"Such a beautiful girl," Lily murmured looking at her.

"Thanks, Lily." Rachel shot a glance at Cort. He smiled.

Rachel's voice filled the air like the comforting aroma of fresh baked chocolate chip cookies. Cort wasn't sure what Rachel wanted to do in her life after high school but he thought it would be a great waste if drama didn't have something to do with it. When she read, he envisioned the scene, heard the characters, felt their emotions.

Priscilla never took her eyes from him as he worked. He reminded himself that she was just a little old woman. It was pure coincidence she looked like she might jump out of that chair and suck his blood.

Even Martin allowed him to give it a go, stating the women had talked about the benefits for days and he was no fool—he'd take benefits anywhere he could get them.

Lily's kind eyes studied him as she listened. Sometimes

her gaze drifted off, clouded over and that pretty smile of hers faded. His heart tugged hard.

When Rachel finally finished and the group broke into talk, Cort neared the end of Lily's massage.

"Such beautiful eyes you have," she told him.

Gently he stroked the gnarled knuckles of her left hand with cream. "Thank you."

"What do you want to do with your life?"

He hated shrugging. Somehow, not knowing shamed him in front of these people who had already lived their lives. "I'm not sure yet."

"What do you like to do?"

"Lots of things. That's the problem."

"That's not a problem." Lily laughed like a bird singing. "My Henry was good at everything too. It makes a man very interesting." She leaned close. He smelled lavender and skin. "It makes a man irresistible." She covered his hand with hers and squeezed.

"Yeah?"

"Henry finally decided to fly planes. We had dreams of going around the world together." She gazed off again, her smile wistful. "Then little Caroline was born and we chose to make a home for ourselves."

"Your daughter?"

She nodded. Cort looked for traces of sadness but saw only traces of an old ache. "She died of pneumonia when she was ten."

"I'm sorry." He swallowed the knot in his throat.

"She was a beautiful girl." Her eyes glistened. Cort had to

steal a deep, silent breath and focus on her hands.

"Does this feel okay?" he asked.

"It feels delightful, dear. Maybe you should be a doctor. You're very kind and gentle. Doctors need that."

"I'm not too good with blood."

"Who is?" Lily asked. "Except Priscilla." She leaned close and looked over at Priscilla who had left the circle and was staring out the dark window into the blackness of night. "She's not afraid of anything. She was a nurse."

"Yeah?" Cort had new respect for the austere woman.

"In an orphanage in Virginia. That's why she never married or had children." Lily leaned back, shook her head. "What she's missed out on. My Caroline was only ten when she passed on but those ten years she was with us were precious. I wouldn't have traded them for anything. Some people never love for fear of losing," Lily shook her head. "So sad."

Cort nodded. Having finished, he eased her hands to her lap where she stared at them, eyes wide with thrill. "They always look so lovely when you finish!"

"They do," he agreed. He looked at Rachel, talking to Martin and Mannie. For a moment he wondered what he should do. Rachel was so at ease. He reminded himself that she'd been at this a lot longer than he had.

Still, he should be able to handle more than a few words with Lily. She gazed off somewhere, deep in thought but her eyes met his.

"Uh," he started. "I'm taking Rachel to senior prom."

Her face broke into a smile. "That's marvelous. And when

is senior prom?"

"In a few weeks."

"You're a lucky boy to take our beautiful girl. I imagine you had to fight for her?"

Cort smiled. Proving that he wasn't some dumb jock had been fun but he'd hardly call it a fight. "She's pretty hot."

"Hot?"

"Uh, sought after."

Lily nodded. "I imagine so. There are so many wonderful things about her. No wonder she's sought after."

"I'll bet you were like that, Lily."

She blushed. "Oh, well. Maybe I was."

He liked that she used Rachel's word. "You know you were."

"A girl can never appear vain."

"So did you go to all the dances?"

"Of course. I used to dance all night."

"Cool."

"We did the Lindy, the swing, the waltz, and I even taught Henry how to polka." Lily sighed. "We were quite the pair."

Another tug gripped Cort's heart, another knot lodged in his throat. He wanted to do something but felt inadequate. His exposure to the elderly had been minimal, his own grandparents living across the country.

"Cort."

He looked from Lily to where Rachel now stood, ready to leave. He patted Lily's hand before he rose. "See you next time. I want to hear more about your dancing."

She cupped his hand in hers. "Very good. Goodbye."

He glanced across the room at Priscilla still staring out the window. Then he said goodbye to the others, promising to return.

Cort and Rachel walked through the quiet hall together, neither looking into the doors opened into rooms. Cort didn't think he could look and see who was inside. There were so many doors.

"You okay?" Rachel asked.

He pushed open the front door, held it for her. "Sure."

Somewhere a spring burn fire scented the air. The sun held in the sky a little longer these days, its red arms reaching out from behind the low westerly mountains as if to grasp for notice as long as it could.

Cort was glad there was a little sun left, something to help with the gloom he felt. He opened the car door for Rachel. Again it amazed him that she'd take the time out of a harried schedule to do something for complete strangers. But then they weren't strangers to her anymore—she'd made them her friends.

He needed to kiss her.

She looked up, her dark hair scattered across her shoulders, blue eyes the color of the blackening sky. The pale nakedness of her lips sent a fast thrum through his veins.

He leaned in the door, taking every second to let his eyes enjoy her face, the way it changed as his neared. Then he kissed her.

Her lips were warm, parted just enough for his mouth to fit over hers perfectly. The kiss didn't need to be long or smothering. He felt a surge of something so deep, nothing but a kiss would express what was inside.

Easing back, he smiled. "Thanks for bringing me here."

"Thanks for coming with me."

He closed the door and went around the car, taking another look at Countryside.

EIGHTEEN

After school, Cort waited for Lizzie in his car. He was supposed to be at Miss Chachi's in fifteen minutes. Tapping his fingers on the steering wheel, he glanced around the parking lot for Rachel's black BMW but didn't see it as cars streamed by.

A tapping at his window took his face to Bree's, peering at him through the glass. She signaled for him to roll down the window.

"Hey. My car's busted. Can I get a ride?"

He wondered where her cavalry of friends was. He knew tons of guys who'd do whatever to give her a ride. "Uh," purposefully he hesitated. "I'm late for work."

"Please," she whined, flipping her striped locks over her shoulder. "Please, Cortie."

He caught Lizzie jogging down the aisle. "I guess."

Bree got in first, then held the seat forward so Lizzie could climb into the back. Lizzie scowled at her as she climbed in.

Bree settled. "Great car. When did you get this one?"

"A long time ago." Cort's voice showed the disinterest he had in any conversation with her.

"Why is she riding home with us?" Lizzie asked point blank.

Bree pulled down the mirror in the passenger visor and looked at herself. "My car died."

Lizzie snorted. "So why not ask one of your real friends?"

"I did." Bree shot her a narrow-eyed look. "That's why I'm here. Cort and I would do anything for each other."

Lizzie sat back on a hacked-out laugh. "Whatever."

Bree faced Lizzie. "How's it going with Todd?"

"I don't even know Todd."

"Wasn't that him I saw you with in Kissing Corner? He looked like the one that was touching you—"

"Okay, shut up right now," Cort said.

"I'm just saying I saw her in Kissing Corner with some guy, Cort. I swear. Two days ago."

"And we gave you a ride because?" Lizzie almost shouted.

Cort swung the car around a corner and onto Bree's street, jamming up the twenty-five mile an hour zone at fifty. Bree clung to the seat.

He slammed the car to a stop in front of the clapboard siding home that was hers. Then he snapped over her lap and flung the door open. "Get out."

"Easy," Bree said. "Ask your sister. It's true. They were all over each other." She got out, smiled and waved. "Bye." She'd barely shut the door when Cort peeled away from the curb.

Cort pinned Lizzie with a glare through the rear view mirror and Lizzie shrunk against the back seat. "Tell me she was lying."

"Um. She was lying?"

"You were in Kissing Corner with Todd?"

"That part was a lie," Lizzie admitted. "It wasn't Todd. I don't even know Todd."

"Who? Tell me, Lizzie. I'll find out anyway."

"Hudson Blair."

Cort slammed on the brakes and the car skidded to a stop in the middle of the road. "Are you out of your mind? Do you know what a—I – I—" Words stammered out. "Lizzie, he's like—the worst. He was on the team with me, and that guy's not even human with girls."

Lizzie's lips curved up. "I'd have to disagree."

Cort whipped around and lunged. The only way he could ease frustration was to beat some sense into her head. But he stopped, slumping over the back seat instead. "Lizzie, he's a jerk. He uses girls like toilet paper. Did anything happen?"

"We just met. Nothing's happened—yet. And if it did you'd be the last person I'd tell. Get over it. I'm fifteen."

"You're a baby." He started the car again, glaring at her through the mirror. "You're not talking to him."

"Yes, I am."

"No, you're not."

"*Yes,* I am."

"Then I'm telling Mom."

Lizzie fell against the bench with a grumble. "You can't. Come on, Cort. You've liked girls who are bad for you, haven't you? What about Bree? I seem to remember when you thought life was over if she didn't like you."

"I've learned a lot since then. People like that are poison."

"That's why you gave her a ride home?"

"I gave her a ride home because it was rude not to."

"And I talked to Hudson because it was rude not to."

"You were in Kissing Corner! People don't go there to do research."

"You hypocrite! I've heard about you in Kissing Corner."

His anger gave way to shock. "You have?"

"Girls have to take numbers."

"That is such crap."

"And you're getting all over me because I'm going to prom with Hudson Blair."

Cort whirled around and the car swerved. "Prom? You are not—no way are you going to senior prom with Hudson Blair. I'll tell Mom what a—"

"Please, Cort, please." She lunged forward. "You can't tell Mom. He's so hot. Do you realize what this would do for my image?"

Cort's glare silenced her, sent her back against the seat with a curse under her breath. He knew exactly what this would do to her image. No way would he let a dog like Hudson Blair within two feet of Lizzie if he had to lock her in her bedroom prom night himself. "I'm telling mom," he finally said.

Lizzie let out a loud, angry sigh. "I'm going whether you or her like it or not." Lizzie folded her arms across her chest. "No one can stop me."

Cort looked at her through the mirror with his lips pinched. *Just watch me.*

Cort dropped Lizzie off and promised he'd tell Mom when he got home from work, since he was late and she wasn't even home yet. Then he jammed to Miss Chachi's, his cell phone in one hand as he drove.

Two people were being retards about prom – Lizzie and Ben. And he knew just how to fix their problem.

"Ben?"

"Dude."

"You asked anybody to prom yet?"

"Not yet. Was gonna soon."

"You're not gonna ask Bree, are you?"

"I am."

"Dude, you can't. She's a loser."

"Beg to differ with you, man. She's totally hot and just because you've been there, done that, doesn't mean the rest of us can't go there, do that."

"I haven't been anywhere or done anything with Bree." Thankfully, Cort thought now. "You've gotta take Lizzie."

"Your sister?"

"Yeah. Come on, dude. She's—" Cort couldn't bring himself to say his sister was hot, that was just plain sick. "She wants to go."

"But…she's your sister."

"I know, I know. You guys are cool, right? You know each other. It'll be fun. She likes you, she told me." A long time ago, Cort thought. But if he could get Lizzie's mind off Hudson, and onto one of his friends he knew and trusted things would be okay.

"She's fifteen."

"And you're seventeen."

"She's your *sister*."

"Come on, you know you want to."

"I want Bree, dude. Bree will… things will happen with her you don't want happening with Lizzie."

Cort gripped the phone until his knuckles whitened. His plan was dying and he was holding onto nothing. He pulled into the parking slot in front of Miss Chachi's.

Cort saw Miss Chachi waving at him from the front window to come inside. "I gotta get to work." He got out, locked the car. "Think before you ask Bree, man."

It was obvious to Cort that Ben could care less about survival; the guy was in it for the moment.

"You late!" Miss Chachi escorted him to his table and pushed him into his chair. He would have laughed had he not been distracted with the prom problem. If Ben took Bree, that meant Bree would be in their group and that would be the worst.

"You have two customers waiting."

Cort glanced up front where Maria de Silva sat in the waiting area. He waved her over, and looked at the older woman sitting next to her watching him. *She must be my new client.* He smiled briefly just to be friendly. She didn't smile back.

"Hey, Maria. What's up?"

Maria sat, extended her hands. "Not much."

"Get asked to prom yet?"

"Todd Doyle asked me."

Cort took her hands, rubbed over her nail beds with his fingers. "Oh, yeah? Is that good or bad?"

"Good. I've only been giving him signals for about five

months now."

Cort picked up his cordless nail file. "Guys can be dense."

"I think he likes Rachel. Aren't you taking her?"

He looked up, nodded. "They're friends."

"Yeah, but he looks at her the way I look at him."

Cort clicked off his filer. "How's that?"

"You know."

"No, I don't."

Maria blushed. Then she leaned close. "All dreamy-eyed and stuff."

"Huh." Cort started filing again. He'd never given it a name but as he thought about looking at Rachel, the way her eyes lit and changed when she looked at him. Was that the way he looked at her? Maybe Rachel looked that way at every guy. "So," he started. "Todd asked you, right?"

Maria nodded. "I'd have to be pretty desperate to ask a guy to prom. I mean, it is a boy's choice dance."

"I know." What he really wanted to know was had Maria seen Rachel looking at Todd that way lately. "You think he likes you? Todd?"

"Probably not. But, hey, I get an evening to try and convince him of what he's missing, right?"

"Right."

She leaned close. "So how do I do that?"

Cort stopped filing for a second, unsure of what to tell her. Truth was, if the guy wasn't interested, an atomic bomb wouldn't bring her to his attention. "You seem to know if a guy is interested. If he's giving you signs, then be friendly and stuff. Go with the signs."

"Hmm."

"If a guy likes a girl, he lets her know," he continued. "Unless he knows she's not interested, and he's just taking whatever she gives him to stay friends."

"I think that's what Todd's doing with Rachel. She seems to have a lot of guys that like her."

Cort didn't like the idea of that. "Yeah." They talked about what Todd had planned for the evening, and for the day date: A trip up the canyon to play at Sundance followed by lunch in the Grill room. The boys were renting a Hummer limousine for the dance. Cort tried not to think about the guys who'd be at the dance wishing they were with his date. Suckers.

He smiled.

The woman walked over after Maria left. She stood at his table, looking at his work area, then around the salon with an inquisitive eye.

"Are you Cort?" she asked, extending her hand.

He shook it. "I am."

"Bonnie Britain." She sat across from him. She looked about his mother's age, he thought. Wore a dark suit like his mother did. Her hair was pulled straight back. She kept a pleasant, half-smile on her face.

"I've heard you're the man to see for nails in Pleasant View." She extended her hands and he looked at perfectly done nails.

"Those look great. Did you just get them done?"

"I want another color," she told him with a little smile. "OPI's Rootbeer Float will work."

"Uh, okay." He stood and went to where Miss Chachi displayed her polishes, took the glazed brown shade and sat back down. He grabbed a cotton ball.

"You like doing nails?" she asked.

He rubbed the acetone-soaked ball over her nails, removing the red color. "Yeah. It's fun. It's been pretty interesting too."

"I'll bet—the only man working with all of these women. I've heard you bring in a lot of business."

He shrugged, felt his cheeks warm. "I guess."

"How long have you been working here?"

"Since it opened three months ago."

"Looks like a nice place."

He glanced up and caught her scanning the place.

"What other services does Miss Chachi provide in the salon?"

"Manicures, pedicures, fills, full sets. Massages."

Her eyes focused on his. "Do you do all of these things?"

Something about the way she looked at him made his face muscles tense. "Yeah."

She nodded, smiled. "How old are you, Cort? About seventeen?"

"Yeah. But I'll be eighteen in April."

"I have a son your age. You a senior this year?"

He nodded, threw away the soiled cotton ball.

"Where do you go to school?" she asked, studying his work permit.

She asked too many questions and even if he wasn't a little kid anymore, the warning he felt inside was there. "PV."

"My son goes to AF."

Probably all lies, he thought. Then he felt stupid. She was a lady, a harmless lady, a new client and nothing else. "What's his name?" he asked and looked right at her.

She didn't even blink. "I get my nails done regularly at the mall. If you're as good as I've heard you are I'll come back."

But you won't answer my question, he thought and decided to get back to work and get this job done.

She left, and gave him a five dollar tip. He'd had bigger, but he didn't expect her to leave any. He couldn't say why.

NINETEEN

Cort tucked another long day with high-pitched gossip under his belt and took the steps up to the back door of home. Inside, the house was dark but for a distant light which meant his mother was at work in her office. He went there.

She still hadn't changed from her suit and he glanced at his watch. Ten-forty-five. "Mom?"

She looked up, slipped the glasses from her nose. "Come in for a second, Cort."

Her tone warned him. He waited in front of her desk. "Yeah?"

"Why didn't you tell me you were working at Miss Chachi's?"

He'd strangle Lizzie. "Liz tell you?"

"No. Back to my question, please."

"Uh. I was embarrassed."

His mother sat back, studied him. Lawyer-mode. "Did you know that you had to be licensed to do nails?"

Cort's heart started to pound. "No."

"Well you do. Miss Chachi, how did she train you?"

"She just showed me. Why?"

"Because she's broken the law, Cort. She's supposed to

hire licensed nail technicians that have gone to school for two years."

"*Two years?*"

"The police shut the salon down tonight."

"What?"

She nodded. "An undercover policewoman broke it today. Apparently your Miss Chachi has done this in five other states, employing under-aged, under-trained people. She was running from one lawsuit in Texas, in fact. One of her employees wasn't properly trained, damaged a woman's nails irreparably and the woman filed a suit."

The blood in Cort's head rushed to his gut. "No way."

"Those girls she had working there? She was taking some of their money off the top for herself."

He couldn't believe it. The woman he'd talked to today— he'd given her a fresh coat of polish and answered all of her probing questions.

"The police will want a statement from you. Don't worry. Although it made me look incredibly foolish that I didn't know you were employed by the woman, I made sure they knew you were innocent. I figured you had to be, you wouldn't have taken a job doing ladies' nails if you hadn't been deceived."

Cort slid into a chair. "I can't believe it."

"I can't believe you never told me."

He looked at her. "Sorry. I was—it was a little lame to admit I'd taken any job I could find." He shook his head. "I should have known. It seemed too good to be true."

"It always is. How was it, anyway?"

"Pretty cool, actually."

His mother's brow lifted. "All those females? I'll bet it was."

"What about the girls? The other nail techs, did they know?"

"I don't know that yet." His mother leaned over her desk when she saw the confusion on his face. "Injustice is everywhere, Cort. You won't see any more money from it. The lawsuit in Texas will eat up any monies left."

Cort slumped back. Prom. He'd have to find another job.

"City council will have a field day with this. Whoever allowed her to set up the business will lose their head, and rightly so."

Cort thought about the revenue Miss Chachi's had brought—he'd helped to bring the sleepy little downtown section of Pleasant View.

"I tried to find you tonight. You didn't take your cell phone?"

He pulled it out of his pocket. The battery was dead. "Dead."

"Where were you?" she asked. He'd be in the frying pan now that she knew he hadn't come clean about where he worked.

"At work, I swear."

Her right brow lifted. "Anything else I should know?"

"I'm going to prom."

"With?"

"Rachel Baxter. She's a cool girl."

"On a scale from one to ten, how invested are you in Rachel?"

"Uh, about a nine point nine."

His mother's smile pleased him. "Very good. Well. Maybe you can tell me how I'm going to break your sister of the delusion that she's going to senior prom when she's only a sophomore. Any ideas?"

"Yeah. Don't let her."

"That's a given. Isn't Hudson Blair one of your football friends?"

Cort nodded. "You don't want Lizzie anywhere near him."

"I've told her no but you know Lizzie. She thinks she's Pollyanna. She'll climb down the outside wall to go."

And get more than a broken back if she goes with Hudson, Cort thought. "She can't go, Mom. The guy's a wolf."

His mother's brow cocked. "She's set on it."

"I tried to get Ben to ask her but he's taking Bree."

"I don't want her going, period. She's too young and hormonal to be alone with any boys."

"I can pick up a new door knob with a lock at the hardware store," Cort suggested lightly. His mother tilted her head with a smirk. "Sorry," he said.

"This is where I want to strangle your father – again," she lamented. "Lizzie needs a man's hand." She shook her head, remorse coloring her eyes.

Cort felt a flash of anger at his absentee father, guilt that his mother had to carry the load alone. "What are you going to do?"

She leaned forward, rubbed her face with her fingers. "Suggest she have a sleepover with her friends and set the alarm with a new code. I don't know. Do you think any of her friends are going?"

He shrugged. He really didn't know what Lizzie and her friends did.

"Well," her mother sighed. "I'll figure something out. I need to get back to these papers. Goodnight."

Cort went right to Lizzie's room. The light shone underneath the door and he didn't bother knocking. She was lying on the floor on her stomach, painting her nails a bright orange shade.

"Hey! You're not allowed," she shot over her shoulder.

"I am when you're being an idiot. That's an ugly color."

"Just because you worked, and I emphasize the past tense of the word, *worked*, at a nail salon, does not give you—"

"I could care less about your nails, Liz." He squatted down next to her. "You can't give Mom a hard time about prom. I won't allow it."

Her eyes narrowed. "And who are you? Last I checked Dad split five years ago."

"Stop it. She's under stress."

"Yeah because she just found out her son was working for a fugitive."

"Cut the drama," he snapped, plopping next to her. "You can't go to prom with Hudson. She's going to let you have a sleepover with your friends and you're going to say yes or I'm going to tell her about your little explorer channel adventure in Kissing Corner."

Lizzie blew on her wet nails so her breath hit him in the face. "Go ahead. I don't give a—"

Cort snagged her wrist. "I'm not kidding."

"Neither am I now let go." She tugged but he didn't release her. "You're going to wreck my nails."

He let go, stood, and smiled. "Fine." Then he bellowed, "Mom!"

Lizzie scrambled to her feet. "Okay, okay. Whatever. What? And you've never been a desperate teenager?"

"I've never been a stupid teenager just asking for it."

"And what if I was asking on purpose?" she shot. He stared at her, his face drawing tight.

"You can ask, Lizzie, I'm not going to say that's not normal—yes I am. You're way too young to be thinking about—"

"Hypocrite, how old were you when you first—"

"I'm still—I haven't—I still—" He couldn't believe he was admitting his virginity to his little sister. But he had to, for her sake. "I've never done it."

She stood utterly still. He expected her to laugh, to tease—something. Her mouth opened without words and in her eyes he thought he saw admiration.

"Really?"

He nodded.

"I would have thought you, well, you know."

"None of my friends have."

"Seriously? Whoa. Even Ben?"

"Even Ben."

She let out a little chuckle. "That's cool, really." The admiration in her eyes was clear. "How come?"

"I don't know. There's never been anybody I've wanted to—sex is serious stuff, Lizzie." And scary, even though he wouldn't admit that. "I don't want you getting used."

She smiled. "It was just a date to prom, Cort."

"Not with Hudson."

She studied him for a moment. "You really think?"

"Yeah."

Lizzie sighed. "But he's so hot."

"He's a creep. A loser. Lizzie, they can line the bathroom stalls with names of the girls he's used."

"Sick."

He reached out and slugged her shoulder lightly. "So, sleepover?"

"I guess," she sighed again. "Of course that will make my friends happy. They all think you're hot. They'll want to sneak in your room and open your drawers. Me, I'll have to be content watching Orlando Bloom movies."

Cort's cheeks heated. "Okay then. Don't give Mom anymore grief."

At the door, he turned and looked at her. He'd never felt such relief. Like his bones could rest. Above anything else, she was his little sister. He'd never see her as a girl. He knew then it would be hard to accept that someday she'd be a woman. All of that could wait.

"Later."

Lizzie grunted.

Magic Hands • Jennifer Laurens

* * *

Miss Chachi's was empty, the 'closed' sign hung in the door. Cort pressed his forehead to the glass and peered in. It looked just like they left it, tidy and ready for another day of business. He wondered what would happen to all of the stuff. A knot formed in his throat. Misu, Tiaki, Jasmine and Abby's faces flashed in his mind. Where were they? What would they do now?

He supposed most of the city had read about the demise of the salon in the Pleasant View Review. The story made the front page for the quiet, cozy city of Pleasant View.

Cort strolled down to Minerva's; a lot quieter now with Miss Chachi's closed. The bell tinkled when he opened the door.

From behind the counter, Minerva smiled at him. "Cort, how you doing?"

The rich scent of chocolate and coffee filled his lungs on a deep, intoxicating breath. "Smells great in here."

She patted the counter. "Come have something." She turned, reached for a white mug on the shelf behind her. "To stay?"

He nodded, pulled out a stool. "Not going anywhere, unfortunately."

"Coffee or hot chocolate?"

"Chocolate."

She poured thick, dark, creamy liquid into the white

mug. "I was shocked when I found out what happened." She slid the mug to him.

"Yeah."

"Did you ever suspect anything?"

He shook his head, brought the mug to his lips. "I can't believe it."

"She seemed like the nicest lady."

A tyrant, Cort thought, but a nice tyrant. He'd not had that much job experience to tell him anything more.

"So you were working and weren't licensed."

"Stupid, huh?"

"Not if you didn't know any better. What'd she do, train you herself?"

He nodded, too embarrassed to look her in the eye, he stared into the mug of chocolate. "I'm usually not that clueless."

Dragging a white cloth over the counter, Minerva chuckled. "You're a male, working in a female world. How could you know?"

His face and ears flashed hot. He sipped again.

"Truth is," she scrubbed a stubborn spot, "we're gonna miss the business your maleness brought down here. Hey, you're not looking for another job by any chance?"

He set the mug down. "Yeah, I am."

"How about you come to work for me? I could use an extra hand."

"Yeah?"

"There's some stocking, minor lifting, stuff like that. If you can learn how to do nails, you can learn how to brew coffee and make hot chocolate." Her smile warmed him with hope.

"Sure, I can do that."

"Super. When can you start?"

"Whenever." He saw prom in brilliant colors again.

Cort left Minerva's with a schedule in his hand for the rest of the month. Not as many hours as he'd had at Miss Chachi's and there'd be smaller tips, if any, but the place was above board and had been in business for ten years.

It didn't take long for word to spread at school about what had happened. Everybody wanted to know. The school paper interviewed him and that was cool, taking his picture in front of the now-vacant spot where Miss Chachi's had once been. The police interview was nerve-wracking but he told them everything he knew and left the precinct with his mind completely clear and ready to move on.

Because it was a Federal investigation, the local police didn't know where the girls ended up. That bugged Cort. In his heart, he couldn't believe any of them had known what Miss Chachi was up to. But then he wouldn't have believed the woman was a fugitive, either.

When prom day finally arrived, Cort was ready for the diversion. He'd saved a nice chunk from his employment at Miss Chachi's and had a week's pay from Minerva's.

He chipped in with Rachel's friends, Todd, Sam, Chris and Pete for the Hummer limousine scheduled to pick them all up at Todd's house for the beginning of the day date.

Todd's house sat in a neighborhood near the high school, behind a sprawl of apple orchards. The house was a one-story brick place with blue shutters and no trees or shrubs anywhere. The half-dozen cars parked out front signaled to Cort he was the last of the guys to arrive. The Hummer was parked and waiting.

He parked his car and Todd dropped out of the door of the Hummer, and waved at him. "We're in here."

Cort jogged over. Todd looked him up and down. "You're late."

"I thought you said one o'clock."

Todd looked at his watch. "It's one-oh-five. Get in."

He wasn't going to get any slack from Rachel's friends, Cort knew that. He climbed in, smiled at the guys all dressed in casual clothes for an afternoon of play at Sundance ski resort.

The reception inside the Hummer was chilly, with the exception of Kevin Mackrel. Cort sat at one end of the limo while Rachel's guy pals sat at the other. Kevin sent him a wave but kept himself neutrally in the middle.

"Put on some tunes," Sam said. Todd dug through his CD case.

"Matchbox?"

"Good Charlotte."

"Blink 182."

"Weezer"

"Keane."

"Heck if I know," Todd said after a while. None of them looked at Cort, or asked his opinion. They finally stuck in Jimmy Eat World, and the inside of the Hummer rocked.

"So we're going to Sundance and then eating in the

Grill room?" Cort refused to be intimidated into silence just because he was out numbered by Rachel's friends.

They stared at him. Todd nodded. "That's the plan."

"Cool," Cort nodded, pressed his fingertips together. "Thanks for letting us come along."

"Anything for Rache," Sam said.

"Yeah, anything," Chris added.

"There'll be tons of deer up there," Kevin began. "Hey, I just got a brain flash. I bet they know how to deal with deer. Yeah, Rob Redford's gotta know something about deer control."

Todd and Sam gave him a tweaked look.

"You still on that, bro?" Cort asked.

Kevin sighed. "Went through bushels of hair and corn cobs dude—didn't do a freaking thing."

When Sam, Todd, and the other guys started talking among themselves, even pulling Kevin into the conversation, Cort regretted not joining Ben and Bree and his buddies for the group date instead—even if it meant watching Ben get eaten alive by Bree. With his friends, at least he wouldn't feel like a cat cornered by a pack of dogs.

"It's cool that you guys watch out for Rachel like you do." Cort decided he'd try to be friends and hope the guys did the same.

They stared at him.

The song blasted all around him, something about it only being in his head that he felt left out and looked down on.

Rachel's friends talked until the first stop at Ticia's house. Kevin grinned, flipped on an interior light and checked out his reflection in the darkened glass window.

"So," Cort started, "you asked Ticia. Cool."

Was Kevin brownie or sunshine?

Kevin wet his fingers, smoothed back a hair. "I'm a lucky man. She's so hot." With that he was out the car and jogged up to Ticia's front door. From the look on Ticia's face, she was ecstatic being with Kevin.

Maria de Silva's house was next. Todd hopped out and went to her door, and came back with a glowing Maria.

Cort had one friend on his side now. "Hey, Maria."

"Cort. Hi." She sat near him, forcing Todd to. "Can't believe what happened at Miss Chachi's," she said as the car rolled on to its next destination.

"Yeah."

"You still going to do nails?" She held out her hands. "Nobody does them as good as you."

The guys stared at him with bullets in their eyes. Cort started to sweat. "Uh, I can't. Turns out you have to be licensed to do nails."

"Oh, too bad," Maria said. "That was about the coolest thing—a guy doing nails."

Todd rolled his eyes and let out a snort.

"Thanks, Maria." Cort thought a subject change was in fast order. "So, you look great." Wrong. The glare Todd aimed at him, warned he was digging a deeper hole for himself.

"Yeah," Todd added, sitting closer to Maria. "You look awesome."

Maria looked from Cort to Todd with a glittering smile. "Thanks."

Cort kept his mouth shut the rest of the drive. As each of the guys' dates was picked up, he merely nodded a hello, watched and listened.

He wasn't in friendly territory.

When they finally pulled up in front of Rachel's house, he was glad to get out. Even more pleased when he saw her, dressed in a black velour sweat suit. She left her hair down under a black and white knit beanie.

He leaned close. "You look great," he whispered.

She smiled and looked over his shoulder at the Hummer idling in her driveway. "Am I the last one?"

He nodded, still in awe. "Saved the best for last."

* * *

After, they lunched in front of a roaring fire in the Grill room, talked about senior year and what life held beyond high school.

Still excluded in most of the conversations, Cort contentedly sat back and admired Rachel in action. She was the center of her friends' world, that was obvious. He didn't mind. Even the girls seemed to focus their attention on her. He liked the way she led talk through diverse subjects. It was more than what his friends and their dates would be doing, that was for sure.

After the day date wound down he walked her to her front door. He leaned in the jamb. "So, I'll be back in a few hours." He couldn't wait to see what she wore to the dance.

She nodded, leaned up. He froze when her lips brushed his cheek. An electric jolt rammed through him and he steadied himself in the door.

"Can't wait," she whispered.

He strolled back to the Hummer with a smile on his face. The guys were silent when he crawled back to his seat. One look out the darkened windows and Cort knew they'd seen the kiss. He tried not to look anyone in the eye as the car started off. It was just him and her friends now, the girls had all been dropped off, and the air thickened around him again.

"Maybe I should take Rachel in my car," he suggested with enough bite in his tone to warn that he'd had enough of what they dished out.

Like a window had suddenly opened, the intensity dissolved. Sam shifted. "No, that's okay."

"Yeah, seriously," Chris added.

Cort looked at Todd, still staring at him. "If you're cool with it," Cort put in, "then we'll keep things the way they are. If not, we ride alone."

A smile broke on Todd's face. "We ride alone? Dude, you sound like John Wayne or something."

Cort laughed with the guys. The night was going to be awesome.

TWENTY

Rachel chose a white dress that sparkled from bust to full hem. A large black bow wrapped under the breast of the dress and tied in front. She wore her hair up in large loops, with glittering sequins sprinkled throughout. She dusted enough sparkling fragrance on her neck and shoulders to glisten like the moon. Then she waited by the front door, trying not to bite the lovely nails Cort had done for her.

She heard the rumble of the long, boxy Hummer and peered out the front room window. Her heart skipped when he emerged from the car, dressed in dramatic black from head to toe. His periwinkle shirt blazed underneath, electrifying his espresso eyes and dark hair.

She couldn't wait to open the door and did, right after one knock.

"Wow." His throat went dry. "You look amazing."

"Thanks." She slipped her arm around his. The gesture had him tugging her close as they walked to the Hummer. Before he opened the door, he stopped. "I have some place I want to take you before the dance if that's okay."

Silver blue moonlight shimmered against his dark hair and black suit. Totally hot, she decided. Irresistible. And he was her date. She'd go anywhere with him. "Sure."

Inside the limo pulsed with energy. Music pounded, laughter rocked. Though the guys took a moment to admire Rachel when she crawled in, the admiration ended there. Cort was relieved that they all paid close attention to their own dates, which meant he was free to lose himself in his.

He put his arm around her shoulders. "This okay?"

"You don't have to ask permission."

Cort noticed the fiery earrings that dropped from her ears. Like royalty, enough to remind him who she was.

"So you gonna tell me my name tonight?" he whispered in her ear.

"No way. You'll have to earn that."

"What have I been doing?" he laughed.

"Proving you're not a jock."

"So this is something else? We're starting over?"

She nodded, her smile teasing.

"No fair whispering," Todd called to them over the noise. Rachel made a face at him.

Cort decided he liked her friends. Where the guys had tested him earlier, that was over now and he felt easy camaraderie. There was one last thing he had to do before the night officially began.

The driver pulled up in front of Countryside Manor.

"Where the heck?" Sam pressed his nose against the dark window. "The geriatric place?"

"We'll only be a second," Cort told them, opening the door. He stood with his hand out for Rachel.

Like a princess emerging from a carriage she eased out of

the Hummer, smiling. "They'll love this," she said. The two of them walked arm in arm up to the door.

"Yeah, I knew they would."

They found their friends in the gathering room. Mannie, Lily and Martin sat around a game table as Mannie dealt a hand of Gin Rummy.

Lily gasped, her hands covered her heart. "Oh, look!" Even Priscilla, standing alone at the window, looked over.

"Lovey!" Mannie steadied to her feet.

"Don't get up." Her hand still in Cort's, Rachel rushed over. She kissed Mannie's cheek and gave her a hug.

"Don't you two look wonderful." Mannie stood back and admired her. "Like a princess."

"Certainly yes," Martin agreed. With effort, he rose and shook Cort's hand.

"How splendid you look," Lily gushed. "Picture perfect. I wish I had a camera."

Rachel took Cort's hand again and tugged him close. "Thank you."

"So you're off to prom?" Lily asked. "Where you'll dance the night away?"

Rachel nodded. Priscilla made her way over, was frowning as she neared.

"Hi, Priscilla." Cort sent her a wave. Her black eyes scanned him from head to toe before shifting to Rachel. She let out a sigh everyone heard. "Proms," she muttered. "I guess they're something to do."

"They're more than something to do," Mannie scolded. "In my day we called them balls."

Priscilla's frown deepened. "Dancing. Who cares? It never did anything for me."

Martin let out a loud huff and craned around to glare at her. "You probably never got asked."

"I got asked plenty," Priscilla snapped.

"When?" Martin demanded. "You were like me, you're still like me—an old fool."

"Phash." Priscilla waved a hand at him. "Speak for yourself."

"Nobody'd dance with you now," Martin mumbled, turning back around.

"Sure they would," Rachel said. "You know how, right, Priscilla?"

Priscilla wagged her head and made a face. "Of course I know how."

"You're taking this young lady out for a proper dinner, aren't you?" Martin asked Cort, as if he was anxious to change the subject.

"Yes sir. A very nice dinner in fact."

"Oh, I love dinner out." Lily clasped her hands at her chest. "It's so romantic."

"Expensive's what it is," Priscilla muttered, loudly.

Martin jerked his head around. "Who asked you?"

"So you're on your way?" Lily beamed.

"We are." Cort's hand slipped from Rachel's, and slid around her waist. "But we can come by later, if you guys think you'll be up."

"You don't want to do that," Mannie told him.

"We'll dance a little," Cort said. "Would you like that?"

"That would be lovely!" Lily's eyes glistened. "I'll have to get ready."

Cort bit his lip. "How about you, Priscilla?"

She shrugged. "I suppose I could stay awake."

"It'd be better than standing over there by that window," Martin said.

"I'll loan you Cort." Rachel swung Cort's hand in hers. Priscilla stared at her.

Martin stood, unfolding himself with a groan. "I'll dance with you, if I can get these legs to move."

"I suppose," Priscilla shrugged, but Rachel caught the surprise on her face, softening the hard lines around the woman's eyes and mouth. She was sure Priscilla was fighting a smile.

Beaming, Mannie linked her arm between Cort and Rachel. "Take pictures—a lot of pictures."

Cort dug into the pocket of his black suit and lifted out a digital camera. "This is a good place to start."

* * *

After Cort took the picture, Rachel hugged each one of her friends, pleased he had thought to share a portion of their night with the seniors. They said goodbye and headed back out to the limo, idling in the street. Music and laughter pumped out from the inside.

Cort's warm hand slipped around hers. She was safe. Her heart was safe. His fingers slowly massaged hers as the two of them walked.

"Mm, that feels good." She closed her eyes for a moment. The warmth of his caress slid up her wrist, along her arm. "That feels really good."

"So good that you'll do anything?" His soft whisper tickled her ear.

She opened her eyes. "Maybe."

He stopped and drew her against him, holding her hands at his chest. His dark eyes glimmered in the moon's light. "Tell me my code name."

Rachel grinned.

ABOUT the AUTHOR

Jennifer Laurens writes novels for young adults from the office of her Pleasant Grove, Utah home. She has six children.

Other Titles:

Falling for Romeo

Nailed

Heavenly

Penitence

Absolution

A Season of Eden

An Open Vein